After the comfortable middle-class background she was used to, Dr Penny
Harcourt didn't find a busy practice in
Liverpool's dockland area the most
glamorous of jobs! But it was only for six
months, and then she would thankfully go
back South again . . .

Lancashire born, Jenny Ashe read English at Birmingham, returning thence with a BA and RA—the latter being rheumatoid arthritis, which after barrels of various pills, and three operations, led to her becoming almost bionic, with two manmade joints. Married to a junior surgeon in Scotland, who was born in Malaysia, she returned to Liverpool with three Scottish children when her husband went into general practice in 1966. She has written non-stop after that—articles, short stories and radio talks. Her novels just had to be set in a medical environment, which she considers compassionate, fascinating and completely rewarding.

The Partnership is Jenny Ashe's sixth Doctor Nurse Romance.

THE PARTNERSHIP

BY

JENNY ASHE

MILLS & BOON LIMITED
15–16 BROOK'S MEWS
LONDON W1A 1DR

First published in Great Britain 1986 by Mills & Boon Limited

© Jenny Ashe 1986

Australian copyright 1986 Philippine copyright 1986

ISBN 0 263 75561 4

Set in 10 on 11 pt Linotron Times
03–1186–57,600

Photoset by Rowland Phototypesetting Limited Bury St Edmunds, Suffolk Made and printed in Great Britain by William Collins Sons & Co Ltd, Glasgow

CHAPTER ONE

DR PENNY HARCOURT climbed the filthy concrete stairs to the fourth floor of Winslow Court—an elegant name for a sad neglected block of council flats. The lift wasn't working, vandalised as usual. But she hadn't intended to use it anyway; the stench inside was too awful. She took a quick sniff at her hanky, masking for a moment the smell of human deprivation by the delicate scent of lavender. She could hear the rain on the roof now. It drummed down with a steady incessance, emphasising the mood of hopelessness all around her. Penny squared her shoulders, and carried on up to Number Seven. The paint was peeling from all the doors, showing the cheap wood underneath, already rotting.

It was almost eleven at night. The answering machine had taken the call: 'This is Dr Zander's surgery. In emergency please call Dr Harcourt at. . .' Penny was tired. But she had been in general practice long enough to be able to ignore it—and she was young and healthy. She smiled a little wryly. All the exercise she got climbing up to flats like this kept her supple! There were no blocks like this in Oxfordshire, where she had done her training. Nor were there so many trivial and irritating calls. One poor soul had phoned her to go and tell off her husband for coming in drunk! Oh well, the weekend was nearly over. She would be off call on Monday, if Dr Zander had got over his attack of Asian 'flu. And the rain might stop.

'I'm Dr Harcourt.'

'You?' The nasal Liverpool accent was immediately recognisable from the one word; so was the disgust at the arrival of a young woman instead of the usual doctor.

'Where's Dr Zander? 'E always comes to our Deb, 'er bein' epileptic an' that.' The man was fifty—looking sixty—with thin unkempt hair, a florid complexion and an unpleasantly smelling cigarette, that curled acrid smoke out on to the dank landing. The unhappy wails of a new baby filled the air, but Penny automatically registered that they were not howls of pain.

'Dr Zander has 'flu. You're Debbie's father? Mr Grant?'

He grunted by way of reply, as though it were a silly question. 'Yer'd better come in. Y'can 'ear the kid. Bin yellin' since six.'

Penny had stopped at the surgery on her way here to check the girl's records. Debbie was a single parent of sixteen, with a baby son of six weeks—not an encouraging start in his little life. But she had read in Leo Zander's small neat handwriting that there was no reason why Debbie couldn't care for her baby. Both her parents were there, and the health visitor had been alerted.

'Hello, Debbie.' The girl was pale and plump. Her long hair lay in lank strands on her rounded shoulders, and was sadly in need of washing. But she bore the tiny bundle tenderly, looking down at the pink face with a worried frown. 'I don't know what's up, Doctor. I don't know what to do.'

'Is your mother in?'

Mr Grant grunted again, at the silly question. 'At the Bingo, isn't she? Always there, she is.'

Penny tried not to recoil as she sat by Debbie on the sofa, and the young mother began to unwrap the greyish shawl, that smelt of urine and vomited milk. 'Babies often cry just because they're uncomfortable. When did you change him last?'

'Me mam did it before she went out.'

Penny controlled herself. The girl needed training in being a mother; it wasn't her fault that she was so woefully ignorant. The crying had eased as soon as the clothes began to come off, stale-smelling and far from white. 'Let me see.' She took him on her knee on a clean towel, and examined him. 'Nothing wrong, Debbie, except for a bit of a cold. Did he take his feed?'

'Yeah.'

Penny looked down at the scrap of humanity, writhing his little legs as though delighted to be free of his restriction. 'He's a darling. Now all I advise is that you give him a little wash, a sprinkle of talc, and a clean set of clothes. I think he'll settle then. Give him a little boiled water and sugar. You're not breast-feeding?'

'No. Me mam feeds 'im.'

'Why? You're his mum, and you're best for him. Remember that.' She watched as the girl began to wash the tiny form. It was very clear that Debbie had no confidence in herself. She still relied heavily on her own mother. The health visitor must help her here. With the right encouragement she could make a loving mother, but the early days were very important. Penny saw that Debbie's eyes were bright with pleasure, as her son gripped her fingers that were trying to dress him gently but clumsily. 'You'll do all right, Debbie. Never give him yesterday's clothes. Keep him nice and fresh, and I'll almost guarantee he won't keep you awake at night.'

'Almost!' Debbie was brave enough to laugh, and Penny smiled with her.

She felt sad on the way downstairs. Sad because there were girls like Debbie, who hadn't been shown by example how to love and cherish a child. This was something she had never encountered in her last practice. She frowned slightly. Here she was, an expensively trained doctor, doing the work of an aunt or a social worker. All that expertise about tropical parasites, about rare bacteria, the mechanism of the inner ear, and the complications of intra-cranial surgery—all that ambition to heal and save life—only to act as nursemaid to people who didn't know any better. Simple standards of hygiene and mother-love had to be taught, like a foreign language.

She shook herself mentally, and turned up the collar of her raincoat as she emerged into the driving rain. It was all experience, and that was what she had come here to learn. She looked back at the square ugly building and sighed for Debbie and those like her. What chance did they have? She checked the sigh as she took her car keys from her pocket.

But the car door was already unlocked. Funny—she always locked it. She opened the door. It was a small Metro, not a fancy car that might inspire jealousy or envy. Yet in the dashboard was a jagged gash where her modest little radio had been ripped out . . .

Penny got in quickly and drove away, her tyres screaming on the corner. She wanted to get away. It had been a long and miserable weekend. She was gaining experience, all right! In two months she had been shown another side to life from the middle-class smugness of her own childhood. She was glad to have seen it; it had made her grow up. But she knew she would never settle here. When her six-month stint was up next February, she would thank Dr Leo Zander politely, and make her way back to the South.

Her landlady was a poppet. She had been lucky to get this flat, above a dental laboratory, with pictures of grinning teeth in the window. It was near the dockside surgery, yet far enough into the suburbs to be free of vandals, and quiet at night. Joanie Fairbrother had a daughter, but she was away at school, and Joanie was glad of a tenant for the back part of the flat.

Joanie would be asleep now. Penny parked the car in the backyard of the lab, and went softly up the stone steps. A late bus went past empty. She sensed, in the dark wetness of the night, the deep grumbling of the engine of a cargo vessel coming in on the high tide to the

Seaforth Container Dock. For a moment the entire city seemed to shudder gently as the boat passed and slowed as it neared the freeport.

Penny went to the window and looked out without putting the light on. The rain had stopped. The tall white lights of the port stood proudly, their rays in tent shapes, lighting up the damp containers already on the dockside. Even the rows of waiting lorries shimmered suddenly, with a strange and unexpected beauty as the white light caught their wetness. Two ships already in dock were lit up, outlined with triangles of light. Beyond them the dark estuary and the sparse twinkle of lights on the Cheshire shore.

She put the kettle on while she checked the answering machine. Thank goodness, no more calls. She began to allow herself to be sleepy. Taking a mug of tea to the bedroom, she flopped on the bed to drink it.

The telephone shrilled in the hall. Penny's heartbeats, just returning to normal, soothed by the sudden beauty of the sleeping docks, shot up again, alerted to Action Stations. She put the mug down and ran to the hall before Joanie was woken by the noise. 'Hello? Dr Harcourt here?'

'I didn't wake you, did I? I phoned half an hour ago, and Joanie said you were out.'

It was the boss—Dr Leo Zander. The strong silent type of man she had known for two months, yet knew she could never know completely. He was too aloof, too self-sufficient. But a good-looking man, with darkish skin, gentle brown eyes that could look very forbidding indeed when the black eyebrows were brought into action. A man she could respect heartily, but never be close to.

'I'm just back from Dourton. Debbie Grant's baby was crying,' she told him. Why was he ringing at this hour? He had a very pleasing voice—nicer over the phone than she had realised. Over the phone you didn't see those eyebrows. 'Everything's all right, isn't it?'

'Yes, Penny. I just wondered what sort of weekend you've had. It's been a filthy night. If you get any more calls, please let me know and I'll do them for you.'

'I couldn't. Your temperature——'

'Been normal all evening.' His voice became slightly more commanding. 'Let me know, please. It is my weekend. I feel I ought to take over, now that I'm better.'

'The rain's gone off. I'll be okay, honestly,' Penny assured him.

'No heroics, woman! I'm awake—and likely to remain so. You sound whacked. I've had years' more practice than you at getting up in the night.'

As usual, Leo Zander got his own way. Penny was displeased—she hated to be bullied. In fact, she liked to get her own way too. She turned as Joanie's door opened and her landlady's pleasant pale face beamed over a blue candlewick dressing-gown that reflected the colour of her gentle eyes. 'Was that Leo? He rang earlier.'

'Oh, Joanie, I'm sorry—I woke you.'

'No, I wasn't asleep. Any tea going?'

'Yes, just made. I'll bring mine into the kitchen and we'll have some together. It was Leo. I'm not sure if he rang out of concern for my welfare, or just to make sure I haven't offended any of his private patients.'

Joanie was quick to defend him. 'He's not like that, Penny. Too many people take him the wrong way—just because he's quiet and doesn't pay many compliments.'

'Sorry, Joanie, but I feel he's someone impossible to fathom. I can't help feeling a bit sorry for him—all alone, and wide awake on a cold wet night in that big house. He's a strange man. I'm sure he doesn't want my pity one little bit.'

'He isn't alone,' Joanie told her. 'His father is still alive.'

'His father?'

'His father. He started the practice. He was a wonderful man. He was a ship's doctor, in the days when Liverpool was a thriving port. He bought a practice on the dockside when he settled down. He was sure his son would take over the practice—and Leo was dutiful. He loved his father. Leo has always done what's right. He's the most honest and true man I've ever met.'

'I suppose I could see that—full of integrity,' Penny agreed. 'But honestly, Joanie, he never smiles. I've never met anyone who never smiles.'

Joanie looked wistful. 'I noticed that. Poor Leo! Sometimes I think his life is ruled by duty. He's so very handsome—but he has no private life at all.'

'I can see that. It was duty that made him ring me tonight. It was duty that made him take me on. He told me frankly that he didn't think much of women doctors, but his patients had said they'd like one. That why I was taken, you know, Joanie—out of Leo's sense of duty.'

'He wants you to stay, though.'

'Joanie, he doesn't! He was so grudging at the interview. I'm on approval—and I know in advance that he'll want to send me packing. He has so little time for women.'

'Don't you think that's a bit of a challenge?' queried Joanie. 'Don't you think that the woman who got through to Leo would be someone very special?'

Penny smiled. She saw in Joanie's face a devotion to the man. It was Leo who had suggested that she might lodge with Joanie. They were closer than she had realised. But Joanie was older than Leo. Surely there was nothing else in the relationship—yet it was clear she was fond of him.

Bathsheba walked across the room and rested her great shaggy head on Penny's knee to be caressed. Penny obliged. 'You're very pro-Leo,' she observed mildly, not wanting to probe. 'So are you,' she added to the bitch, as she wagged her tail at the comment, as though she understood it.

Joanie smiled. 'We haven't had Bathsheba all that long, you know.'

'I know. She's scarcely a teenager yet.'

Joanie nodded, and stifled a yawn. 'We used to have a golden Labrador. I called him Pharaoh because he was so stately—a dear old thing.' She was silent for a moment. The whirr of a helicopter filled the silence, as it patrolled the river. Bathsheba lifted her ears, but recognised no threat, as the sound of the rotors faded as it flew north towards Formby Point.

'What happened to Pharaoh? Old age?' asked Penny.

'No, much worse. He was poisoned.' Joanie swallowed as she remembered, and her voice was husky. 'Probably burglars. They feed poisoned meat to clear any danger to themselves.' She looked down at Bathsheba, and her expression cheered. 'If you'd seen Leo then, you'd never have doubted he had a heart. He cared for the old boy as though he'd been human—sat up with him all through the night. That wasn't duty, Penny—it was love. I didn't want Pharoah taken to the vet, I knew I'd never see him again. But Leo got something from the vet to help him sleep, to take away the pain or something. Then he sat and stroked his head until he—well, he just fell asleep.' She shook away a couple of tears. 'Oh, Penny, if you'd seen him! I just know he died happy—because of Leo. There was such trust in his eyes . . .'

Penny murmured something, but Joanie wasn't listening. She went on, 'The next day he went to work. But when he came back from morning surgery, he had Bathsheba with him. She was small and cute. Gemma just held her and hugged her, and we both fell in love with her.'

Again there was a silence. Then Penny said, 'Okay, he's okay. We'd better get some sleep, Joanie.' She stood up. 'But okay or not, he doesn't want a woman.' Joanie yawned. 'Go to bed,' Penny advised. 'Doctor's orders.'

'I will. But he does want you, honestly—I'm sure.'

'He told me that Liverpool was a stupid place for a woman to work.'

'I suppose it is. There are dangerous areas.'

'He didn't like it when I said I intended to pull my weight equally. I've done it so far. But tonight was a bit of a shock.' And Penny confided that her radio had been stolen. 'I suppose I've been lucky not to have had any hassle before now. Two months have been trouble-free.'

'Well done.' Joanie yawned again. 'Sleep well, Penny.'

'No problem.' But she lay awake for a long time, worrying over Leo. Why had he said he wouldn't sleep tonight?

There was the usual Monday morning confusion in the waiting room, spilling over into the corridor and right out into the street. The pavement was littered with dog dirt, discarded chewing gum, empty crisp packets, and chip papers, blowing around doing a melancholy ballet in the chill breeze.

Penny edged past the queue to get to her own boot-cupboard of a consulting room, past humanity in varying states of cleanliness and body odour. She heard Kay Phillips, the senior receptionist, trying to keep order in the corridor, where the scene was more like a wrestling match. She and Judy Flanagan were doing their best to take people in their proper turn, whipping nimble fingers along the shelves, sliding out record cards and putting them in four trays, one for each doctor. In between, they answered the telephone, and grumbled to each other that they hadn't had time to put the kettle on.

'Another normal Monday, Kay,' said Penny, as her pile of cards was brought in.

Kay pulled an expressive face. 'I don't know how we carry on without a nervous breakdown!' She seemed ready to go on complaining, but there was an angry protest from outside Penny's door, and she turned to see what was happening. Penny heard her voice—penetrating as she said because she had to keep order, and there was no other way. 'Will you please keep to the side so that we can get past! Fiona Wood, go back to your own place! Mr Atkinson, you know very well that you mustn't bring Sherry inside—least of all on a Monday. Go and tie her to the lamp-post—I'll keep your place. Harry Arnold, what are you doing here? How many times have I told you not to come for your injection on a Monday morning? Mrs Sanderson, you must wait your turn. I know Dawn is ill, but so is everyone else, or why the heck would they be standing here like lemons?'

Someone protested at the length of the queue. 'I've got to get to work!'

'Lucky you, havin' a job to go to.'

Then Kay: 'Dr Harcourt's list is shortest. I'll send you to see her.'

Penny heard him grumble. 'Them young ones? Nah, I don't want to see her. Put me for Dr Richards, then.'

Someone further back laughed. 'I thought you liked young women, Derek.'

'Aye—the ones y'can tek out for a drink. Not them snotty types.'

'She's not gorra bad figure.'

'Better than my old woman's, eh?' And a chorus of laughter. Penny pulled her white coat firmly round her, and wondered how ill Derek really was. The laughter seemed pretty healthy, though it was followed by a few chesty coughs.

It was a drab little room, Victorian still, though attempts had been made to brighten it. The window frames were solid brick, and the glass was the original frosted stuff, that made Penny feel shut in and caged. How far away was Oxford now—that leafy lane where the modern surgery where she did her training nestled among lilac and cherry blossoms. What a long time ago that seemed. And how far away . . . Nobody had taken the radio from her car there.

There was a sudden piercing scream outside her door. It was a genuine cry of pain. Kay put her head round the door. 'Doctor, it's Dawn Sanderson. She looks bad. Can I get her in to see you?'

'If that was Dawn screaming, get her on the couch at once.'

Kay and Mrs Sanderson carried the girl in. She was about seven, and she was crying and holding her stomach. The mother was one of those tiny under-nourished women, common in Merseyside, to whom life seemed an endless and intolerable burden. She was permanently crouched as though expecting life to be rough to her. Now her white face was scared, as she looked down at the tense body of her daughter. Dawn cried out again at the pain, and drew her legs up towards her body. 'I can't get her to lie flat, Doctor,' said her mother worriedly.

Penny examined the abdomen. There was immediate guarding as the muscles tightened, then the crying turned to an unhappy moaning, as the child instinctively knew Penny was trying to help her. 'How long has this been going on?'

'She was bad yesterday, but I thought it was something she'd eaten.'

'I thought so. Bowels? Constipated. Yes, I think this is her appendix, Mrs Sanderson. I'll get her admitted at once.' Penny pressed the buzzer. 'Ambulance, Kay. Dawn to be taken to Admissions—surgical. Get me the surgical registrar next.'

The child was carried out by kindly ambulancemen, who coaxed a smile from the tearstained face by calling her 'Your Majesty' as they wrapped her in a red blanket. Penny filled in the diagnosis on Dawn's card while she spoke to the surgical ward. 'Right, Kay—next, please.' She reached for the next card. 'Good morning, Mr Allsop.'

Mr Allsop glowered uncertainly. 'You don't look old enough to——'

Penny cut him short; she had heard that too many times. She recited her answer. 'I've been qualified for five years. I got Honours in medicine, did three years' general practice training, and I don't often make mistakes.' Her voice was cutting, to emphasise her authority. 'Sit down, please. What can I do for you?'

'I just feel tired all the time.'

That was a typical complaint. Now all she had to do was discover whether he were genuine or a malingerer. 'Could you strip to the waist, please.'

'I only need a tonic, Doctor. I'm——'

'Shirt off, Mr Allsop. Tiredness could be due to all sorts of diseases. You want me to find out, don't you?'

Meekly he obeyed. She checked him thoroughly, and dismissed him without a prescription, but a diet sheet and advice about taking more exercise. Mr Allsop was not amused.

Outside the door, while she could still hear him, he grumbled, 'I'm not going to her again. Thinks she knows it all, she does!' Penny smiled. He would probably get the same treatment from the other partners. Leo had stressed the need to educate the patients to take more care of themselves. If Mr Allsop went to another partner, he would find they supported her line wholeheartedly.

Penny found that she was beginning to get to know the 'regulars'. She enjoyed her work. For all the many coughs and colds that turned up, there were always one or two cases of real medical interest and challenge. She heard Kay close the door at ten-thirty, and then go and answer it when latecomers rang the bell. 'Well, it wasn't my fault the bus was late.' 'I had to get me mam's bread before I come.' 'I overslept.' Kay always made it very clear what she thought of these excuses.

After the last patient had limped out with a note to go for a replacement of his surgical corset, Judy was quick to bring in a steaming mug of coffee along with a pile of repeat prescriptions. 'And Dr Zander asked me to give you the list of calls.' She handed over a small paper.

'Right—thanks, Judy.' Penny pulled the list towards her. 'Only four? I don't believe it! Not on a Monday.'

'Dr Zander said you were late last night. The others are taking more,' Judy told her.

'Hmm.' That wasn't pulling her weight. She was quite capable of doing her fair share, but somehow she didn't insist on equality at that moment. It was nice of Leo Zander to be so thoughtful.

There was yet another shrill of the front doorbell. Penny heard the click of Kay's shoes along the corridor, the door opening—and then she heard Kay cry out. She ran to the corridor. 'What is it, Kay?'

A youth in tattered jeans and a dirty damp pullover had pushed past Kay, and she was running after him, trying to pull him back. 'He's after drugs, Dr Harcourt. He's half crazed, doesn't know what he's doing. We've been told not to supply him—he gets a ration from the Centre in town. He's wanting them to sell to other people. Stop him, Judy!'

He had stopped, and had turned to Penny. It must have been the white coat that attracted his attention. He held out a clenched fist towards her. He was a good-looking lad, but Penny recognised the glazed eyes, the set expression from what she had been taught when she was doing Casualty in London. 'Are you one of our patients?' She wasn't afraid.

But Leo had come out of his room now, seeing off his final patient, and he was quick to take in the situation.

'Ah, Neville, so you've come to see us again. I hope it's to tell us how well you're doing at the Centre.' His voice was unruffled, as he took the lad's arm and led him —suddenly pliable and co-operative—into his room. 'You haven't forgotten that promise we made? About trusting each other implicitly?'

Dr Richards and the other partner, tall, silent Dr Santani, left the surgery together. Penny was just going, when she remembered she had to ring the insurance company about her car radio. 'Kay? before you go would you just get me the medical insurance people?'

And so it was that the senior and the junior partners left the surgery simultaneously. They emerged into the corridor at the same time, and Leo Zander courteously opened the front door for her. The cruel wind was lurking outside, tossing dirty newspapers and litter with a grim playfulness. Penny looked out, then back at the corridor floor, trodden with muddy footprints and stubbed-out cigarette burns. She turned away, suddenly disgusted.

'Not a pretty sight, Penny?'

She turned to look up at him, tall, and strangely unmarked by his busy morning. His neat grey suit looked brand new, his white shirt shone in the dingy corridor, and his shoes showed no spot, as though he walked through different streets from mere mortals. He closed the door and checked that it was locked. 'Neville might be watching,' he explained.

They walked towards the cars, parked at the kerb —his dark blue Rover, and her small grey Metro. He said gently, 'I apologise for the environment.'

'It isn't your fault,' she told him.

'No.' His dark eyes searched her face. 'It isn't these people's fault either. They didn't choose where they were born.'

Penny protested, 'They choose whether to drop litter, though.'

'Could they? Who taught you?'

She managed a smile. 'Oh, all right. I'm sorry, I didn't mean to be critical.'

'Penny, you're a good doctor. When you know my patients really well, I think you'll be an excellent one,' he told her.

She turned and stared. This was the man who had told her at her interview that he had no time for women doctors. 'Well, thank you.' She looked behind him, where the brass plate proclaimed 'Dr L. Zander, Dr D. M. Richards and Dr C. Santani.' Could she ever see the addition of her own name underneath, on this draughty and windswept corner of dockland? The grey reality of James Street loomed all round her, and she felt frightened of it happening without her permission.

Leo Zander hesitated, as though not sure whether to prolong the conversation. Then he said, 'Well, see you this evening, Penny.'

'Yes. Goodbye.' She would have liked to talk more, but could think of nothing to say. She got in the car, pulling a face at the empty gap where the radio was, and looked again at the list of calls she had stuffed in her jacket pocket.

There was a shout farther up the street, and Penny looked up to see a large woman in a floral overall and scuffed carpet slippers running with clumsy gait along the windy street, her face distorted with fear. 'Doctor —Dr Zander! Oh, please come. It's Tim, the window cleaner, 'e's fell off of 'is ladder. 'E isn't moving!'

Penny got out quickly and locked her door. Leo was already striding along with the woman. He turned to Penny. 'Call an ambulance, Penny,' he said tersely.

'Okay. What number house?'

The woman turned. 'Thirty-six. 'E was doin' next door to me. God in 'Eaven, I 'ope he's all right!'

Even in the haste of the moment, Penny was impressed by the way the woman relaxed as soon as Leo

turned to her. There was something in his very presence
that calmed her, inspired trust. And she was an admiring
onlooker as Leo supervised the lifting of the unconscious
man by the ambulancemen, and the administration of a
tranquilliser to the upset woman.

They walked back along James Street. 'You all right,
Penny?' Leo Zander asked.

'Yes, thank you.'

'I'm glad you took Joanie's place. At least I know
you'll get a good lunch.'

'I'll do the calls first,' she told him.

'No need. I gave you the non-urgent ones, repeats.
Just check that they're all right. It will do on your way
back this evening.'

'Okay.' She didn't thank him again, though he was
enormously thoughtful. But she felt that if she wasn't
careful he would be taking away her decision to be an
equal partner in this practice—for as long as she was
there. There was a tendency in this good-looking and
increasingly interesting man to treat her like a child. It
was something that Penny knew she must watch, other-
wise he would never take women seriously. And that
was her aim, in the few short months left in Liverpool.

She watched his car disappearing into a side street. He
was hard to know—hard to like, perhaps, because he
was always right, always so sure of himself. But it was
very easy to admire and respect him—and Penny
allowed herself to be grateful she had met him. And that
she would only know him for six months. That was the
length of time she felt she could put up with someone
who was always right!

CHAPTER TWO

'You mean to tell me you've never been to a drug lunch?' Dai Richards didn't believe Penny. It was later in the week, and surgery had been quiet. The four partners were drinking their coffee in Leo's room, surprised at the bonus of having time for a chat. 'Well, why not come along with me? The rep will be delighted, so will some of the other GPs. A new and lovely face to brighten the monotony!'

Chris Santani shook his head. 'Don't go with him, Penny. His bad reputation might rub off on you.'

'I wasn't going anyway.' Penny wasn't sure if she ought to have accepted Dai's compliment; it irritated her. 'They try to buy the doctors' goodwill with alcohol.'

Leo looked up from the pile of letters on his desk. 'A very accurate diagnosis. I agree with you, Penny.'

Dai disagreed. 'There's no obligation. Of course, they hope you'll go away with the name of their products ringing in your ears, but you don't have to.'

Chris said unexpectedly, 'I might come along, Dai. Lalla isn't feeling too cheerful today. The kids are playing up a bit because my brother-in-law is staying with us, and he spoils them.'

'Oho—the first steps on a slippery slope for a married man!' Dai was a bluff and cheerful man, who seldom took anything seriously.

Chris shook his head. His glossy black hair was always neatly cut, his three-piece suit almost dapper. 'No, Dai, don't get me wrong. I just look on it as a free meal. Let's go.'

'Right, mate.' Dai put his coffee mug down. 'How about Father?'

Leo turned at the use of his nickname, and smiled. 'I won't be bought, thank you, Dai.' He finished reading the last letter and laid it on the pile. 'And don't think it's because I'm a prig either. The conversation bores me stiff.'

Penny looked down at the dark head of her boss, and found herself smiling at his dry comment. Perhaps deep down Leo was a bit like her—sure of what he liked and disliked, and unwilling to be pushed around.

Kay Phillips came in with the call book. 'Can I have Father's letters?' She covered her mouth. 'I'm sorry, Doctor, I didn't mean——'

Leo looked up. 'Don't apologise. Only I'm not sure if this nickname refers to me as a father figure, or a father confessor. Which do you think?'

Kay had been with the practice a long time. She grinned. 'Both, Doctor.'

Leo stood up and straightened his back. 'Right, which of you is seeing Mrs Williams?'

The others had already taken the calls they wanted. Penny said, 'She's on my list.'

'You haven't been before?'

'No. Is there something I should know?'

'I don't think she'll last very long. Be kind to the relatives. I had a chat to them last week, but it's very hard for them to watch her. They're a close family.'

'Cancer?'

'Carcinomatosis.'

'Does she know?'

Leo said slowly, 'I think they always know at this stage. But she's never asked. She understands that we've done all we could.'

'Poor lady! I'll go now—unless you feel you ought to see them?' Penny pulled on her sheepskin jacket and picked up her case.

'No, I'd like you to go.' There was something unreadable in his dark eyes as he looked down at her.

'Penny!' Dai called after her as she made her way along the corridor, 'The lunch is at the Dog and Partridge, if you feel like coming along later. You might be glad of a stiff gin.'

'That's very thoughtful of you, Dai. 'Bye.' As she got into her car Penny reflected how easily the medical profession could slip from sincere compassion to light-hearted banter. To an outsider it could sound heartless. But Penny knew how very necessary it was to be able to cut off from human suffering before it became too much to bear.

Mrs Williams lived in a small terrace house near the city centre, just off the main road. It had only recently been modernised, and a toilet put indoors. They were small and uninspiring. But it was easy to see the ones whose owners cared for their homes. Mrs Williams' front door was new, the curtains were spotless, and the outside had been painted with stone paint. 'The boys done it,' she explained, 'They've been very good to me.'

She lay in a bed in the corner of the front parlour. She was hardly there, yet there was a brightness in the blue eyes that defied description. 'They're wonderful boys. You're new, aren't you, dear? What a pretty girl!'

Penny swallowed hard. 'I'm Penny Harcourt.' She took the thin hand that lay limply on the coverlet.

'That's Kevin, my youngest. That's Gordon—he's the clever one. And Stephen—he's the eldest.' Penny could see why her patient's eyes were bright. She was bursting with pride in her sons. How very alone they would feel without her loving spirit in the little house. The atmosphere in the darkened room was hushed but very calm. There was a scent of eau de cologne coming from the embroidered pillowcase. Mrs Williams was clearly very weak, but she was anxious to talk. 'Do you want to examine me?' she asked.

'I'd better see how your blood pressure is doing, if you don't mind.'

'Of course. And Dr Zander usually has a listen to the old ticker. That's what he calls it—the old ticker. He's been so wonderful. I'll never forget what he's done for us. He's always popped in when he was passing this way. Just to see his lovely face round the door made me feel better—a hundred times better. To think he'd taken the trouble to think of me!' Mrs Williams had spoken too much, and now had to stop, and take in great gasps of air. Penny patted her hand, and waited until she was calmer before getting out her sphygmomanometer. She wondered if Leo didn't want to see the patient die. Was that why he had sent her today? Or did he just want her to meet the family? She would ask him.

There was a tap on the front door as Penny was reading the blood pressure—pitifully low. She heard a murmur of conversation, but did not turn round until she had completed her brief examination. She looked at the transparent skin over her face, the blue eyes still with that light in them. 'You're in no pain, Mrs Williams?' she asked.

'I ache, love—I ache all over. But I can bear it, thank you.'

'Mother, it's t'Vicar.'

A slim young man, not much older than Stephen, came forward, and after smiling and nodding at Penny, took her place at the old lady's side. She whispered something, and he turned and said, 'She'd be very grateful if you'd pray with us, Dr Harcourt.'

'Oh. Oh yes.' There was no time to be selfconscious, as she saw the light in the old eyes begin to dim and darken. The familiar words flowed round them, as Penny tried to control her tears. 'Hallowed be Thy name . . . For ever and ever . . .'

She sat in the car afterwards, unable to start it until her eyes had gone back to normal. There was a gentle tap on the window, and she looked up to see the young clergyman. He wore a tweed jacket over his clerical collar, and slim-fitting trousers. His hair was brown and boyish, falling over one eye in a wave. Penny managed a smile as she wound the window down.

'Are you all right?' he asked.

'Yes, thanks.' She put her hanky away.

'I'm Robin White,' he introduced himself.

'Penny,' she smiled.

'Penny, I wonder if I could diagnose that you need a drink?'

'What?'

He smiled, and pointed across the road, where a red brick public house was just opening its great iron grille. 'Join me?'

'All right.' Why not? It was true, she could do with a drink. The youthful Vicar was right.

The wind had dropped at last, and there was a feeble sun trying to break through, livening the dismal uniformity of the streets. There was even a misty-blue view of the two cathedrals on the skyline, with the tall Beacon distinctive between them. Robin White saw her looking at them, and smiled. 'The square one is the Anglican one, the cone is the Catholic one. They're at opposite ends of Hope Street. Read into that what you like.'

'They're really rather beautiful.' She had stopped to gaze. 'It reminds me of Oxford. I do miss it.'

'So do I.'

They exchanged a smile—something in common. Penny said, 'The Sheldonian——'

'Magdalen tower——'

'Little Clarendon Street——'

'St Giles by night.'

He took her elbow and led her to the mighty oak bar. 'What'll you have?' There was no one else in except two youths in jeans, and a small ex-mariner with a black patch over one eye.

They spoke quietly in a corner niche. Penny relaxed in his company. Robin didn't preach or talk religion, but she felt he was a deeply committed man, and as such, had a calm joy and acceptance of his life, and it helped her. She felt comforted after they had talked, almost optimistic.

As they parted, Robin said, 'Let's hope we meet again.'

She smiled at him. He was only about four inches taller than she was. 'That would be nice.'

''Bye, Penny.'

She had to pass the surgery before going home, so she thought she might as well fill in Mrs Williams' BP and heart rate. Robin was going to call again that evening, but she had a feeling that it might not be necessary. Except that the boys would perhaps be glad to see him . . .

There was the sound of a key in the lock. There was no evening surgery tonight. Chris was on call, so it must be him. Penny called out, 'Hallo? I'm in the office.'

The voice that answered her was not Chris's; it was Leo's. He said, 'Yes, Penny. I saw your car.'

He came into the office. It was small and cramped, and they inevitably stood quite close together. 'Did you go to the Dog and Partridge?' he asked.

'No. I had a ham roll at the Liverpool Arms in Cherry Street.'

'That was a good idea. How was she?'

'Going calmly.' Penny felt discomfited suddenly at his closeness. 'I say, I've finished in here. I'll get out of your way.' She pushed the drawer shut.

'No hurry,' he told her.

'But don't you want——?' He couldn't have come in just to see her.

'I saw the car. I wanted to know if they minded me sending you?'

'No. They were terribly sweet to me.' She felt a lump in her throat again. 'The Vicar came. We—prayed——'

'Nice people.' Leo perched himself on the edge of Kay's desk. 'You didn't feel it was too much?'

'Of course not. Leo, I have done my training. I've seen more than one person die. You mustn't treat me like a—' she couldn't say child—'like an idiot.'

'I wouldn't dream of it.' But he clearly wasn't expecting her to tell him off like that. 'And if you were an idiot I wouldn't have taken you on.'

'Sorry.' Penny looked away. 'Are you always right, Leo?'

'Yes. I've got it down to a fine art.' She wasn't sure if he were joking, his face was so grave. 'Was your last senior partner like me?'

'Nothing at all like you,' she assured him.

'Better or worse?' He was looking almost human now, as he teased her gently to own up. The dark eyes were gentle and warm.

Penny looked into them with a touch of defiance. 'Different.' She didn't intend to give anything away. She would keep herself as unknowable as he was. 'Are you going to sit there all night?' she added.

He seemed to remember why he had come. 'Oh yes.' He eased himself off the desk. 'I came for a book Chris lent me. It's in my room, I think.'

Penny gave an involuntary shiver. The surgery wasn't too cold. She wondered if it was anything to do with the fact that they were standing very close together. But Leo was solicitous. 'I say, I'm sorry—I shouldn't keep you talking. The heating has been off since midday, and it's cold.' He stood back so that she could leave the office first. She couldn't help brushing against him as she left, catching a scent of the man—a combination of his suit, his starched shirt, the warmth of his body. He looked around him as he switched off the light. 'Let's leave the place to its own friendly ghosts,' he smiled.

'There must be hundreds of those,' Penny observed.

'You're right. This has been a surgery since the time of Queen Victoria. If there are ghosts, then they've seen a lot of drama here.'

'Joanie told me your father bought this place.'

'That's right, yes. He loved the place—and the people. He used to write snatches of his memoirs in longhand before . . . Maybe one day I'll make a book of them. He'd like that.'

As she drove back to Joanie's, Penny tried to figure Leo out. He had chatted perfectly frankly—yet he always managed to keep himself out of the limelight. She knew very little more about her enigmatic chief, yet she had this nagging feeling of pity for him. Why? He was the most self-sufficient man she had ever met. He wasn't even going home to an empty house. It was luxurious —she'd been there when he interviewed her. And his father was there, plus a cook-housekeeper and a handyman, a married couple who went every day. He had no need of pity. He was just a cold fish who did his job well—and somehow managed to get his colleagues to do the same.

Dai Richards, on the other hand, was the most open and likeable man she had ever worked with. She was still mystified, however, when that evening Dai rang Joanie's bell and asked to speak to Penny.

'What are you doing here, Dai? Don't tell me your date has let you down?'

'Not on your life! She can't wait for me to show up. But I wanted a few business words with you in private, my lovely Penny, before I go. You haven't got a drink, have you?'

'There's some sherry. Medium?'

'Yes, please.' He accepted a glass, and sat down, looking, for Dai, rather uneasy. 'The fact is—' he stopped, and smiled suddenly, 'I say, are you sure you can trust yourself with a handsome Welsh devil like me? One medium sherry and I'm all yours.'

'Pull the other one,' laughed Penny. 'I've seen your girl-friend and she's lovely.'

'Correction—you've seen one of my girl-friends. Safety in numbers.'

'Well, it's time you settled down, in my opinion. You'd better realise that all that beer is ruining your figure. Soon you'll find that not even a second-hand Porsche makes up for a vanishing waistline.'

'Ah, now you've hit it—what I came to talk about. The Porsche . . .'

'Yes. Go on.'

'I've sold it.'

'Good. I always thought it was too expensive and showy to drive round the Dock Road doing calls.'

'Ah.' Dai stopped. 'I really could do with your advice, Penny.'

'I'm no agony aunt,' she protested mildly.

'No, child, but you've got a head on your shoulders. It's about money.'

'Oh dear!'

'You might well say that,' sighed Dai. 'I've bought another car.'

'Well, I know nothing about cars, except that they make a noise, take you from A to B—and if you live in Liverpool they get stolen fairly often.'

He looked at his watch, stood up, and paced up and down the room. He was getting a little stout—but when that happened he usually gave up beer and took up jogging. He was over thirty, ruggedly good-looking, with a rather untidy mop of chestnut hair. With a rush of confidence, he said, 'Penny, I've used a surgery cheque as a down-payment on an Aston Martin.'

She looked up in astonishment. There was nothing to say. Even the rather skittish Dr Richards that she knew couldn't do such an impulsive thing, surely?

'Say something, Penny!' he urged uncomfortably.

'The surgery account. . . Are you going to get it back?'

'I can't. It's done now.'

'So what on earth can I say? I'm only very junior.'

'Yes, but you could be supportive, Penny. Put in a good word for me. I'll pay it back as soon as I can, but there's a slight cash flow problem . . . I'll pay it back, you know that. But it might take a bit longer than a month.' Dai held out his arms appealingly. 'You all know how much I've wanted an Aston. It suddenly turned up – the exact one I wanted. I couldn't let it go, Penny. I had the signed cheque with me for some new instruments. So bang—I did it.'

'Bang,' she agreed automatically. 'Well, I can't see that I can do much——'

'Wait till you see the atmosphere turn blue when I tell the others!'

'Why can't you pay back any sooner?' she asked.

'Because I have a large overdraft.' Even when confessing his sins, Dai had a winning way of appearing confident that all would be well. He put down the empty sherry glass. 'Well, thanks for listening. You didn't exactly come up with understanding and sympathy, but I've put you in the picture, and that's what matters.'

'Hmm,' she mused. 'You've almost made me into an accessory after the crime.'

'Oh, don't be like that!'

She watched him go, looking out of the window to see and admire the elegant silver car that meant so much to him. She didn't have any strong feelings about using surgery money—but Leo was different. It wasn't right, and Leo was pretty hard on anything that wasn't scrupulously correct. The accounts were a model of precision. She smiled sadly. Poor old Dai!

It proved to be longer than he thought before Dai owned up. The wintry weather had started the cold and 'flu season early, and every surgery the following week was crowded to bursting.

Penny knew all the regulars now. Indeed, most of them came to see her from preference, because she usually had the smallest crowd waiting. But Fiona Mather, the mentally retarded girl, came because she worshipped Leo, and would wait for him all day if need be. Herby Allsop, however, became a regular—he came because it was somewhere warm to sit and read his paper. So he cunningly started to keep to Penny's diet, and insisted on seeing her regularly for a weigh-in and progress report. There was Harry Atkinson, who had bad asthma, but wouldn't hear of parting with Sherry, his little black bitch. And she was a darling, and Penny agreed with him, merely advising him to wear a mask more often in the house. Sherry was his only companion.

Then there was Jack Sayer, with diabetic retinopathy, whose sight was going and who came for moral support. And Mrs Sanderson. Her Dawn had recovered well from her appendix operation, but her mother had developed agoraphobia and only went out of doors when she knew she was coming to the surgery, only minutes from her own front door. Debbie Grant's little Jamie began to thrive, but he had a tendency to coughs and colds, and so Debbie was a frequent patient. And after little Mrs Williams died, Penny found that her middle son, Gordon, started coming along, taking days off his hairdressing business with vague aches and pains which Penny diagnosed as hidden depression.

Life had become busy, and Penny spent her days off sleeping, or chatting with Joanie. She got into the habit of taking a walk with Joanie when she took Bathsheba for a walk. It was cold and windy most days down at the beach, but they felt invigorated when they returned to hot soup. Joanie talked a lot about her daughter Gemma, and Penny got the feeling that she was worried about how to cope with a rapidly maturing teenager. But

Penny didn't offer advice; she knew it was a private affair, and she didn't want to appear to meddle.

One Friday, at the end of a hectic week, they were almost ready to leave morning surgery when there was a loud ring at the bell. Penny heard Kay saying, 'I'll go, Judy, it's my turn. What cheek, coming after twelve!' Penny smiled, Kay had a cutting line in insults for latecomers. But there was no cutting retort. She heard deep voices, worried voices, and when she went to the door she saw two large police officers standing in the office, while Kay feverishly rifled through the files and the stock cupboards.

'What is it?' Penny asked.

'Oh, Dr Harcourt, these men are from the Bootle Station. Some prescription pads were found on a rubbish heap in Litherland. They think some known addict had stolen them, and thrown them away when he knew he was going to be searched.'

'What's the name on them?'

'It's Dr Santani's name.'

Penny looked up and down the corridor. She said to the sergeant, 'I suppose Dr Santani's is the easiest room to get into, when both the girls are busy in the office. It's the nearest to the door.'

'Is there anything of yours missing, Dr Harcourt?'

'I'm pretty certain nothing is.' She was fairly meticulous when it came to locking cupboards and drawers. 'I only get one pad at a time out. And I keep it in my bag.'

'We'd be glad if you'll check,' said the sergeant politely.

'Of course.'

'And we'd like a word, please. I'd like a list of all your known addicts.'

'I personally haven't treated any. Dr Zander would know.' Leo was still seeing a tail-end of patients. The police moved ponderously into Chris's room and closed the door. Penny said to Dai, 'I feel like a criminal.'

'Don't take any notice, flower. It's the way they've been trained to speak. Anyone can see what an innocent young thing you are.'

Penny forced a smile. 'Well, I suppose it is a serious matter.' She made a quick list of her calls. 'I'd better set off, it's a long list today.'

One of the policemen came out of Chris's room. 'Please don't leave yet, Doctor. It's important that we question all the staff.' Penny sat at her desk, irritated at the waste of time. She could tell them nothing; it was Leo who counselled these patients, built up a relationship of trust with them. Dai joined her in her own room while they waited.

It grew late. Leo finally finished surgery, and came out to the rest of them sitting glumly about. He quickly fetched the list, and dismissed the others. 'My staff are above suspicion,' he said firmly. The police took his word meekly. 'Some practices might have guilty secrets, but not this one, Sergeant,' Leo assured him.

Penny stole a glance at Dai, who looked very uncomfortable. Chris said, 'Drugs is a nasty business. But it's profitable for people who want extra money.' Dai positively blushed, and turned abruptly towards the window. Penny felt sorry for him. Things could be a bit rough if the police found out about his overdraft and big car, and the Aston was parked quite noticeably in the street outside.

Penny went over to stand by Dai. He muttered into her ear, 'Why do doctors have to be bloody saints, man?'

'Because ordinary people put their lives in your hands.'

He looked out at the patches of blue sky showing above the hard slate roofs and the dark outline of the local gasometer. 'It's not going to be a bad afternoon, I hope.'

She smiled up at him. 'Cheer up!'

They were permitted to go as soon as Leo had given

the police a few addresses. Penny said to Dai, 'You see? It does pay to be always right. They believed Leo because he's always kept his reputation scrupulous.'

Dai looked mightily relieved. 'I'm beginning to see his point. But what a strain, man, to keep it up twenty-four hours a day. I don't think I can manage that much piety. I wonder how he does it.'

She said mischievously, 'Maybe he turns into Mr Hyde at night.' They left the surgery laughing, hearts lighter than perhaps Dai deserved. But Penny knew he was a good person underneath. Cars were his only addiction—and that wasn't a criminal offence.

She was tired that afternoon, and went to her room to lie down for an hour. But as soon as she had kicked off her boots she heard the phone go. She wasn't on call, but she sat up and waited. 'Penny?' called her landlady.

'Yes, Joanie. Is it for me?'

'Leo for you.'

Leo. What could he want? He must have a call about one of her patients. 'Hello, Leo,' she said cautiously.

'You looked rather apprehensive this morning,' he explained, 'so I thought you'd like me to come round and explain what happened.'

'That's very nice of you.' He could tell her over the phone, surely? Or was there really something he dared not say? 'See you shortly, then.'

Penny walked around nervously before he arrived. She poured herself a sherry, then decided that was bad manners, and she ought to wait and see if her visitor wanted one first. She frowned at herself for being so jittery just because the boss was calling for a chat.

Joanie ushered him in, and Penny wiped her palms on a handkerchief. 'There isn't anything wrong, is there?' She didn't mean to burst out with the question. She'd meant to be cool and collected, to offer a drink, to wait for Leo to explain himself, but her guilt at knowing Dai's secret made her blurt out the words.

Joanie closed the door. They were alone. Leo was looking relaxed and natural. 'I hope you don't mind me popping in,' he apologised. 'No, there's nothing wrong. They're going away to check the list. I'm pretty certain it wasn't any of our patients. I know them all pretty well, and they trust me.'

She swallowed. 'He was very suspicious of us.'

Leo smiled at her, his dark eyes not a bit forbidding at this moment. 'They're a suspicious lot—it's their job. But don't worry, I doubt if they'll be back. They'll just check all the practices in the area, and interview the known addicts. Problem over. Chris is going to take more care of his cupboard in future. He thinks it must have been left unlocked some time last week.'

'So the affair is over?'

'I'm pretty sure it is.'

Penny tried to suppress a sigh of relief. 'Would you like some sherry?' she asked.

'I'd love it. Let me get it.' He went over to the sideboard. 'I say, this is the one I have.' And Penny felt ridiculously pleased that she had the same taste in sherry as the great man. Her heart stopped fibrillating, and she leaned back, feeling much better. Leo lifted his glass. 'Here's to the law.'

'Must I drink to them? Oh, all right.'

Leo laughed. 'I must apologise for Liverpool. It must be a bit much to take in, in two months and one week.'

'You know the actual dates.' She smiled. 'No, I'm getting used to life here quite well really.'

'I hope you don't mind me coming,' he said again, and Penny looked at him curiously. Surely Leo Zander hadn't lost his self-confidence?

'No. It's very nice of you.'

'I felt like a drive out. I get restless sometimes—don't know quite what to do when I'm on call. Reading is fine, but occasionally one feels like a change.' He shifted in his chair. 'Do kick me out if you feel like doing something else.'

'Maybe you ought to take more exercise?' Penny suggested.

'One can hardly go jogging with a bleep stuck in one's tracksuit,' he pointed out, and she had to agree. 'I even thought of trying one of those appalling drug lunches for a change. What do you think? Would you come if I arranged it?'

'Perhaps.' She was flattered to be asked. 'But if you like, you can take Bathsheba for a walk. That's what I do when I feel restless. She's a lovely dog, and so affectionate.'

She offered him more sherry, which he declined. 'Maybe I'll come next time you take the dog, then.' And after a few more trivial exchanges, Leo stood up to leave.

Penny walked with him to the door. 'It was nice of you to come.'

He turned and looked down into her face; he seemed to be searching for the right thing to say. 'I didn't like seeing you so upset this morning,' he said.

'I'm fine now.'

'Good.' And to her amazement, he took her arm gently, bent towards her, and kissed her lightly on the cheek. 'See you later, then.'

Penny stood for a long time gazing after him. She didn't quite know why. She ought to feel outraged—but somehow she didn't.

CHAPTER THREE

I⟶ was the middle of the following week before Penny was alone with Leo Zander again—time enough for her to have forgiven him for the sexist slight of having kissed her on the cheek. She had realised it was nothing, and tried to forget it. So when he called her into his room at the end of Wednesday's surgery, she entered with no real annoyance left. If ever there had been . . .

'Good morning, Leo.'

'Morning, Penny. I've something important to ask you. You aren't in a hurry, are you?' He had been sitting at his desk, but he rose when she came in, with a rare show of good manners.

'Not a bit. Only two calls each.'

'I was wondering if you'd come with me to see a couple of my private patients?'

'The posh end of town?' Penny was nothing if not direct, and Leo seemed to have got used to it by now. 'Your end?'

He smiled slightly. 'Yes—my end. But the Donaldsons came from this end. They were good friends of my father's, and they loyally stayed with me when they could have transferred to a practice nearer their home.' He looked at her with a slightly superior look, as he explained away her prejudices.

She wasn't too cowed; she was getting used to Dr Zander. 'Why me?' she queried.

'Penny, you're very suspicious of my motives. Well, I'll tell you. I think you're more like me. Dr Richards is always in a hurry, which isn't very thoughtful. And Chris shows too much reverence for their money, and that isn't the way either. I think they'll like you.'

'That's a compliment,' she smiled.

'Is it? It's only the truth. You see, I might want to take a week off. I know winter is a bad time, with heavy surgeries and lots of 'flu. But I have a friend in Paris who's been bothering me to visit her since summer. Now the Donaldsons aren't well—they're both in their eighties. So I'd like to be sure I can leave them in good hands. Satisfied?'

'All right. You want me to come now?'

'Please.' Leo collected his overcoat. 'The house is one of the big ones on the front overlooking the Marina.'

'It would be.' But she smiled as she said it, and Leo Zander didn't retort. She followed his Rover down past the docks, and towards the north end of town. The suburbs became leafier, the houses larger. He finally turned into a winding drive that led up to a grand entrance, with large wooden doors with elegant brass-work round the knocker and bell.

Penny parked on the forecourt, where there was room for half a dozen cars, and joined Leo as he rang the bell. 'Gosh, it's cold down here!' she shuddered. The wind was fresh, and very cold, making Penny shiver in spite of her sheepskin. She waited, expecting a grand butler, or at least a serving wench—but no. Shuffling footsteps could be heard, and a plump homely woman with apple cheeks, an apron and carpet slippers opened one of the great doors with a wince.

'Leo, my love, come on in! It's good to see you.'

'Hello, Lil. That arthritic shoulder playing up again?' He bent and kissed her cheek. 'This is my new partner, Penny Harcourt. She's going to practise on you.'

'Nice to meet you, my dear.' Penny got a kiss too, and a warm smile from the little lady. 'I'm Lil Donaldson. My husband is Sam. And neither of us would still be here but for this kind gentleman.'

Penny couldn't help taking to Lil at once. She looked around at the high ceilings, ornamented with carvings and touched up with gold. 'What a lovely house!' she exclaimed.

'Yes, isn't it?' No false pride either, just a genuine comment. 'I always dreamed of living in a big house, but I never thought I ever would. It was Sam's business that did it. He has a good head on his shoulders, has Sam.'

'Let's have a look at the old man,' said Leo. 'How's his puff lately?'

'He's not so bad, thank you. Come on through, I'll put the kettle on.' She called, 'Sam, it's Leo. Are you decent?'

'No, lass, and I'm too old to change now.' A wheezing old voice, but full of laughter. Sam Donaldson was lying on a window seat, a checked rug over his legs and a black beret on his white head. 'Hello, my old friend. It's nice of you to spare the time for us—I know how busy you are in the winter.'

Leo introduced Penny. Sam said, 'Old people are a nuisance, love, but there's nothing we can do to turn the clock back. Thanks for coming.'

It was so utterly different from what Penny had expected that she was a little stuck for words. But Lil soon had her chatting as though they were old friends. She brought in a silver tray with tea and home-made scones, and they all sat round while Leo examined hearts and blood pressures one by one. 'You're both pretty well, but your ankles are swollen, Sam. Have you been up and about?'

'No. I've been as good as gold.'

'Then I wonder if I ought to increase your medication. Penny, what do you think?'

'It might be a good idea. Try it for a day or two.'

Sam chuckled, 'She's got a head on her shoulders too!' He motioned to Penny to help herself to scones. 'Excuse my hat, but I can't get used to a house with double glazing. When I see the waves whipped up like that—' they saw through the picture window a great vista of angry water, lashing the sea wall on the opposite side of the road. 'It's psychological. I feel better when I wear a hat.'

'It suits you,' said Penny.

'Well, thank you for that. And what do you think of Liverpool? Leo was very doubtful if you could manage —especially in Dourton. There's some pretty rough types out there.'

'I'm managing fine,' said Penny. 'But I do know what you mean. Dr Zander is slightly chauvinist still, and I have to convince him that I can take a fair share.'

Lil was wide-eyed. 'You go out in the middle of the night to Dourton?'

'Well, I've only been three or four times,' confessed Penny, 'and last time my car radio was stolen, but I can put up with that.'

'Well, well!'

Penny frowned. 'Lil, there are dozens of women doctors on Merseyside. Why shouldn't our practice have one?'

The old people turned to Leo for an answer. 'They've got one, haven't they? My only objection was that my area is a bit rough. I admit freely that Penny's brain is first class.'

'I should hope so!' Lil staunchly backed Penny. 'You're one of those men who look on women as tender little things. Have you counted how many in your area work when their husbands can't get a job, come home and cook for a family? They don't complain about their aches and pains, their coughs and colds, their rheumatics. They carry on, spend a lifetime of sacrifice, a lot of them. Stronger than the men, I say.'

Penny smiled, but didn't give Lil the round of applause she would have liked to. She knew Leo would have taken the point; he had been listening intently, his eyes on the little lady who held forth so vehemently.

'I hope you're going to stay, Penny.' The old man's

eyes were sincere. 'I hope you can put up with us all. We're a funny bunch, but we mean well, us scousers.'

'I know that.' She tried to avoid the question, but Lil asked her again. 'Well, I've got to decide by February. And so has Dr Zander.'

'He's decided.' Lil was certain. 'You know how I know? Because he's brought you here, that's my opinion.'

Leo laughed heartily. 'Lil, you're priceless, and I love you! But we've taken enough of your time. Here's a prescription, Sam. Take an extra half a tablet for a day or two, and give me a ring if the swelling doesn't go down.'

'Thank you, lad. Your dad saw my dad out, and I reckon you'll do me the same favour. Thank you, Leo.' And he shook the younger man's hand with warmth.

'Lil, I hope you've told me everything. Rheumatism under control? Breathing giving you no trouble?'

'I'm right glad you've got a lady partner. Maybe I'll tell her my troubles. If ever I get any,' Lil added. And she said to Penny, 'If that's all right with you, love.'

'Here's my number.' Penny saw something in the twinkling grey eyes that alerted her sixth sense. 'Don't hesitate, any time.'

'Thanks, love. I know you're on approval, but even this perfectionist here couldn't find a fault with you, I'm sure.'

'He's a hard man to please.' They all laughed, as Penny and Leo went to the door. But she felt a little embarrassed at the open discussion of her future. She had already decided that her stay here was going to be no longer than six months. She liked the people now, but a grey, dull city was not for her, with all the litter, the crime and the deprivation. Six months was the limit. Lil made her feel guilty for wanting to leave. And she had noticed that Leo had made no commitment either.

Leo stood in the blustering wind for a moment while

Penny got into her car. 'Well, now I know they're in capable hands,' he said.

Penny smiled. 'Either of the others would have been just as capable.'

He gave her a knowing look, but made no answer to that. 'Thanks for coming, Penny.' And with a wave, he left her.

It was Chris Santani who drew their attention to a subtle change in their chief. 'Father's been particularly amiable lately,' he remarked.

Dai agreed. 'Very goodnatured—almost human.' He sipped his coffee. 'Had you noticed, Penny?'

She couldn't answer. 'I didn't know him before. He's always been the same to me—very proper, but very helpful. It was only at the interview that he frightened me a bit by his stern look.'

Dai grinned. 'Then we must put the improvement down to feminine company!'

'Don't you dare!' They were both aware of Penny's dislike of her sex being mentioned, and she knew they only did it to joke. She became aloof, and looked through her call list. Her professional side was alerted. 'What's the matter with Gordon Williams?' she asked.

Kay had taken the call. 'He just feels bad—muzzy, he said. I asked him if he needed a call, and he said yes. You know that family never call us without a good reason.'

'That's true.' Penny was convinced that Gordon's troubles were all in his mind. He was grieving for his mother, and couldn't cry like a woman could. But she must see him; she knew the danger of taking one diagnosis for granted.

He was sitting on the sofa with his head in his hands when she walked in through the door that had been left open. 'Gordon, what is it?' she asked.

'I wish I knew.'

'Is it just depression, do you think? You are grieving.'

'No, it's not that.' Gordon was irritable. 'She was

dying long enough for us to get used to the idea. It's nothing to do with that. I'm just off colour.'

'I'll send you along for some tests. Now, let's have a look at you.' There was nothing to find on physical examination. Penny wrote out some forms for blood tests and an X-ray. 'Take these to the Royal. Come and see me next week, when I'll have got the results.'

'Thanks, Doc.'

She drove away, sure that her original diagnosis was right. Gordon was closest to his mother. Only time would help him.

She drove slowly along the shabby streets, her thoughts with the family she had just left. She looked absently at the monotonous terraces of houses. Only three more months until she could choose a practice with leafy lanes and thatched cottages to visit. That was something to look pleased about.

Last call. Penny drew up to check her street map. It was a bad area, all right. Even the street names were defaced and unreadable. She wondered if anyone had actually died because it had been impossible to call an ambulance, all the phones being vandalised. And such were her thoughts in that grim part of the city that she thought the patient who was lucky enough to die would be better off in Paradise than stuck here in these mean streets.

She started the engine, and turned in the direction she thought was the correct one. She drove slowly, as she searched for street names.

A child playing on a tricycle suddenly got off and ran into the road directly in front of Penny's car to pick up a dirty blue hair ribbon. Penny gasped and jammed on the brakes, swerving round the little figure, who was oblivious of the danger. Thank goodness she was only going slowly. She jumped out of the car, but there was no need. The little girl had run back to her trike.

The mother ran out of the house then, suddenly

scared at the screech of the brakes. 'Our Carol, you're supposed to be looking after Marie. What the hell d'you think you're doing? That child might have been killed!'

An older girl had appeared round the corner. 'I was only at the shop.'

The mother swore at her then, and Penny closed her eyes in momentary distress. Little Marie was dressed in a cheap cotton dress—but it was the dirt on it that demonstrated a mother who didn't care. It wasn't only today's dirt. Carol, the schoolgirl, wore a tight skirt, and white socks with high-heeled sandals. Her hair was dyed orange, and spiked up in points. The mother wore tight jeans and a crimplene sweater that had once been white. Her high-heeled shoes badly needed heeling, and her hair was dirty, held back by a rubber band. There was a smoking cigarette in her hand, and a packet of twenty in the jeans pocket.

Penny drew Marie towards her. 'Let me make sure you're all right, dear.' The child looked at her with huge blue eyes. There was no harm done. 'Better stay on the pavement, Marie,' Penny said gently.

She said to the mother, 'She's a lovely child.'

The resentful expression cleared a little. 'Yeah.'

Penny wished with all her heart she had the guts to tell her to clean the child up, wash that pretty gold but matted hair. Instead she said, 'Her hair's lovely. Have you tried her with Zena shampoo?'

'That stuff? Couldn't afford it.' And the woman drew another cigarette from the packet, lighting it from the butt of the old one, which she threw casually into the street.

'Really?' Penny looked pointedly at the cigarettes, furious indignation bursting inside her. But what was the point? She could do nothing. She went back to the car.

The woman went indoors without another word, leaving the peeling door ajar. Penny looked after her, and sighed. It was painful to see such waste, such neglect.

And it was tragic to see how the mother gained no pleasure from her own children. How could she? Yet the answer was quite obvious. She had probably been ignored in the same way, her own mother out at work, finding children a bar to her own pleasures.

'What a very nice surprise!'

The words were so diametrically opposite to what Penny was thinking that she started in surprise. She had been reaching for her safety-belt, ready to drive off. Now she let it go, her spirits suddenly lifted by the sight of the young Vicar, Robin White. He stood on the pavement, dressed in tweed jacket and polo-necked sweater, where he had just emerged from a back alley. 'Hello, Robin,' she smiled.

'Are you still busy?' he asked. 'Or can we repeat our lunch at the Liverpool Arms?'

'I'd love that. Can I meet you there in ten minutes?'

'Lovely.'

Robin was sitting in the corner where they had sat last time, two glasses of bitter and two ham rolls already on the table. She joined him, sitting down with a deep sigh. 'You sound positively fraught, Penny.'

'Down but not out.'

'Tell me about it.' His voice was so very calm and soothing, his darkish eyes so piercing and kind. Here was someone who understood—and someone who knew the very depths of deprivation, yet who could still be optimistic about humankind.

'You do me so much good,' she smiled, pouring out the tale of the young child so beautiful, who would grow up lax and uncaring, like her own mother. 'And I ought to have told that woman to stop smoking. I'm just a coward. I heard how she could swear at her own daughter.'

'Bad day,' sympathised Robin.

'Let's just say that Liverpool isn't for me,' Penny sighed.

'Lucky you to have a choice.' His voice was quiet, but his words passionate.

'Do you want to get out too?' she asked curiously.

'I could. I was offered a parish in Wales, but I turned it down.'

'But——'

'I have no choice. My conscience wouldn't let me leave.'

She looked into his face. 'You make me feel very small and mean.'

'Oh, Penny, I didn't mean to. Your job is quite different from mine.' He looked into her eyes. His face was almost bright with faith, his curly hair falling over one eye, his personality magnetic. She felt his attraction like a physical pull. They stayed still for a moment, gazing at each other. It felt warm and good. Penny felt a stirring in her body that was unfamiliar to her, but she knew what it was, and she made no attempt to suppress it. What was the harm in a little gentle falling in love?

That evening, there was an atmosphere in the surgery. Penny couldn't put her finger on it, but the air was frigid, and not with cold. Kay was short-tempered and sighed deeply when asked to do anything. Afterwards, Dai was very subdued, as he drank his coffee in a corner, looking with great interest at a print of the Albert Dock on Leo's wall.

Leo, as usual, took not the slightest notice, but went on making his notes until he finished, when he lifted his neat head and sipped his coffee. Penny watched him, but made no comment. It had been a traumatic day for her too, and she would be glad to get back to homely little Joanie and her Lancashire hotpot.

When Kay burst into tears after being asked to get yet another phone number for Chris Santani, Leo looked across. Penny thought she saw concern under those black brows, but his voice was matter-of-fact. 'Time of the month, Kay?' he asked.

Penny burst out then, 'That was sexist! Do you say that to all women who are upset?'

Leo raised an eyebrow. He was getting used to Penny's outspokenness, but that was pretty tough. 'Not all of them, Penny. But Kay does have a problem. Her menopause is a bad one.'

'I see.' Penny was in no mood to apologise. But she felt herself beginning to blush. And she realised that her own irritability today could indeed be put down to the same cause—pre-menstrual tension. She bit back any further comment. Leo was clearly in one of his cutting moods.

When they left the surgery, Dai whispered, 'It's all in the open now. I've finally confessed all.'

'Well, you landed all of us in it this time,' said Penny ruefully.

'What's that supposed to mean? I thought you were on my side.'

'Just being in your confidence doesn't put me on your side.'

'Oh, Penny, Penny! And I thought you loved me,' he sighed.

'When are you going to pay the money back?'

Dai shook his red head, his beaming smile proclaiming the opposite of his words. 'Ah, now I know where I stand. I've fallen from grace.' And he turned towards his lovely silver car with an expression of great affection. And she couldn't help but smile at his almost childish joy as he got in.

'Good night, Dai,' she said.

She drove home, again irritated by the lack of a radio. She must go ahead and get it done. It was nice to listen to music when she was feeling bad. Leo had again been right. He had told her he had it down to a fine art, and he had not been joking. He irritated her too. Thank goodness for Robin and his calm gentle friendship. Of all the people in Liverpool, Robin was the best. Her mood lightened at the thought of him.

Joanie was another calming influence. As Penny opened the front door, there was Joanie in the kitchen, where a delicious smell made the homecoming even better. 'Oh, Joanie, am I glad to get home!' Penny exclaimed.

But as her landlady turned round, she saw with dismay that Joanie's eyes were red and her face blotchy. 'Hello, Penny. How was the surgery?'

Penny went into the kitchen and sat down on the stool by the little table. 'It was tiring, and the atmosphere was horrid. But if you have a problem I'm all ears. That is, if you want an ear. If it's private, then I don't want to know.'

'Was Leo in a good mood?'

'Leo? Not particularly overflowing with the milk of human kindness.'

'Would you like some soup? Or will the hotpot be enough?'

'Hotpot—and stop stalling! Do you want the benefit of my opinion or not?'

'I do, very much, Joanie assured her. 'You see, there's something you have to know about me.'

'Fire away.' Penny helped herself to food, while Joanie sat opposite her and folded her hands on her knee like a tragedy queen.

Just then Bathsheba heard Penny, and hurled herself into the kitchen like a great bear. Penny said, 'A dog is so good for one's self-esteem, Joanie. Just look at all that devotion and affection!' The bitch wagged her tail so forcibly that Joanie had to pull her round to her own side of the table. She wagged her tail there too, and wafted a paper off the table. Penny picked it up. It was a letter, and she saw the heading—The Francis Smythe School for Girls. That was Gemma's school. Without meaning to, she caught scraps of the letter. 'Very disruptive and anti-social behaviour. Next step will have to be expulsion.' Expulsion. . . . Penny looked up into Joanie's woebegone face.

'Read it,' said Joanie. 'It came this afternoon.'

Penny read it, then she looked up. 'So they want you to take Gemma away.'

'I was afraid it would come to this. They've warned me before, but Gemma told me it was only one mistress, Miss Dartford, who was picking on her. This doesn't look like just one mistress.'

Penny looked back at the letter. 'How old is Gemma?' she asked.

'Fourteen.'

'Mmm. Has she any problems that you know of?'

'Only the biggest—I should have told you before. She's illegitimate.'

Penny said briskly, 'That's an old-fashioned word. Well, let's see what we have to do next. Does she want to come home, or would she like to stay at that school?'

'I honestly don't know.' Joanie wiped her eyes. 'I'm afraid I don't know her very well. I'm ashamed of it, but I don't know quite how to handle her.'

'You love her, don't you?'

'Yes, of course I do.'

Penny said firmly, 'Then it's only a matter of time. You'll pull through.' But she wasn't sure. She had never seen Joanie like this. Poor Joanie! She would never have thought such a kindly soul could have this kind of problem. And why had Joanie asked how Leo was? What did he have to do with this?

'It's so hard to know when to be strict, and when to give in. I do so want her to be happy, but she doesn't give me the chance—she's cheeky, and she acts so grown-up sometimes. To me, fourteen is an insecure age.'

'It is. But nowadays they want to show you it isn't. It needs a lot of tact. I've got a patient of sixteen with a baby, two years older than Gemma. You see, their bodies are ahead of their minds. They need help, but hate to ask for it.'

Joanie looked miserable. 'I can admit it to you—I'm terrified of half-term. I don't want it to be all shouting and misunderstanding. But I know it will be. It's happened before.'

Penny could see now that she was being asked for help. 'Maybe I can talk to her. I can sympathise with you both, because I've been to boarding school. It did upset me, to be sent away from home—I thought they didn't love me. I could perhaps help you both to understand each other.'

'It would be a miracle, after reading that letter.' But Joanie did look a bit more cheerful.

'I agree. But miracles do happen.' Penny had realised the necessity of a positive approach, after talking to Robin White. Dear Robin! He had helped her a lot, just by being himself, natural and optimistic. Her mind wandered for a moment.

'But I'll have to tell Leo,' Joanie said.

'Why?'

'Well—' Joanie looked down, and toyed with the letter before her, 'it's important to him.' She looked as though she was going to reveal more, but came to a full stop. Then she looked up, with brimming eyes. 'Thanks, Penny. I feel better now that you know all about it.'

'But I don't . . .' There was a block there now. Leo's part in this was taboo; that was obvious from Joanie's silence.

CHAPTER FOUR

PENNY and Joanie talked far into the night. Joanie seemed glad to be able to be frank. She was frank about her love affair, frank about her dread of responsibility, totally frank about her love life—but totally silent about the name of the father of her child.

At ten, Penny went out for fish and chips. It was partly because she was hungry, but more because she had to do something to stay awake. When she came back, Bathsheba rushed to welcome her, to land her considerable weight on Penny's stockinged feet as she curled them up on the sofa. Jade, the green-eyed black cat, nestled against her. Penny stroked the sleek creature absently, as she heard again the familiar tale of sudden passionate attraction, ignorance of contraception, of later decision that the love was not strong enough to last. And so Gemma was born without a father to give her a name, and was cared for by Joanie and Joanie's parents, until they also passed away.

Penny caressed Jade's aristocratic chin. 'I'm only a child in terms of experience, Joanie. I won't mind if you think I've no right to comment.'

'You go ahead. Why do you think I told you so much? You know it all now, Penny.' Joanie's tired pale face crumpled, and she turned away. 'Oh, Penny, I feel so sorry for that kid. What can I do? Expelled! I'd never have thought . . . She was never disruptive here. In fact she was very quiet.'

'Have you ever thought that she wants to be expelled? Wants to come home and stay with you? You're all she has, Joanie, and she might treasure it.'

'Unless she thinks I can't afford the fees. I never told

51

her that—someone else foots the bill . . .'

Again Penny saw how intent Joanie was on keeping the name of Gemma's father secret. 'Does she know that she ought to feel grateful for being sent to the Francis Smythe? She might resent that—having to be grateful when she doesn't really enjoy it.'

'I've told her how lucky she is,' admitted Joanie.

Penny hesitated, as she saw suddenly how tired and old Joanie was looking. The kind blue eyes were dull, the fine lines showing around them. 'Oh, Joanie, I'm so terribly sorry!' she exclaimed.

'Help me. I don't know what to do.' Joanie's voice was quiet, but she was on the verge of tears.

Penny said slowly, choosing her words, hoping she wasn't giving offence, 'I always wanted to come home at the beginning of every term. I hated being sent away. It was better when you were used to it.' She paused, but it was plain that Joanie was depending on her. She tried again. 'I wonder if Gemma really wants to be expelled, wants to come home, to stay with you where she knows she's loved? She might be wanting more signs of affection from you?'

Joanie scoffed. 'Gemma's hard as nails, never shows affection. Never the sort to make any fuss, give anyone a kiss, that sort of thing . . .'

'Are you sure? Do *you* do it?'

Joanie turned away, pushed at Bathsheba's great bulk. 'Move over, dog, you're too heavy!' Her face was impassive now. 'I'll make us another pot of tea, I think.'

They drank hot tea, and Penny made no further reference to Gemma. But Joanie suddenly burst out with, 'You could be right, Penny. I never thought about it. I don't know my own daughter—never really felt that she confided in me. I kidded myself that that was because there was nothing wrong, but now I think she hid her private thoughts from me. I must be a rotten mother!'

Penny said quickly, to prevent any more tears, 'Don't feel too bad. It's not too late, you know. She's only just growing up. When she comes at half-term, you can get to know each other again.' Secretly she prayed that Gemma would be willing. How could she know the girl's real character?

'I don't know how. Oh, Penny, I know I was wrong to send her away. I can see now it was just selfishness on my part—letting someone else take the responsibility for my daughter. I shouldn't have done it. But it seemed so sensible at the time. And I had the money . . .'

'From her father?'

'No.'

Penny said quickly, 'I'm sorry—not my business. But if I were you, I'd have a word with the schools here, ask if they'll take her. Then explain that if she wants to stay at home, you don't mind.'

'It's such a big step,' fretted Joanie. 'I'm not used to a teenager around. I'm sure I won't be able to cope.'

'You will while I'm here. I'll help—unofficial aunt!' Penny did her best to be positive. 'Let's try and make it fun for all of us.'

'You make it sound easy.' Joanie looked down at her hands, twisting together in her lap. 'I have tried, you know. I've tried and failed.'

'This time it'll work,' Penny assured her. 'When you tell her about the new school.'

'And what if she hates the idea? Or they won't take her?'

'They'll take her. A mother wanting her daughter to be near her—they'll be very sympathetic.' Penny sounded more sure than she felt. 'Now I must get to bed.'

'I've kept you up,' Joanie apologised.

'And why not? An important daughter like Gemma is worth it. You'll see—we'll sort her out, you and I.'

'Thanks.' Joanie seemed to have shrunk, a pathetic

figure now in the corner of the big sofa. Bathsheba
rubbed her head against Joanie's knee. 'I'm glad you're
here, Penny love.'

Penny slept fitfully, tired though she was. Joanie's
problem was a big one, and Penny felt that it had become
hers now, on top of her commitments at work. She was
too involved—and yet what else could she do?

Her dreams began to mix up all the cases, all the
problems she had coped with in the past weeks. And she
seemed in her dreams to be searching, searching for
someone to help her. She found herself stumbling over a
muddy ploughed field, her feet sinking, bogged down in
the furrows. And there at the edge of the field was a tall
dark figure, holding out a hand to aid her. But the more
she struggled, the farther away the figure became, the
outstretched helping hand. She couldn't see it now, and
she had not been able to see its face . . .

The feeling came back to her when she was next at
work. In flashes, between patients, she was tempted to
put a face to that shadowy figure—she almost knew it
must be the compassionate face of Robin White. She
wondered if he would mind if she got in touch. But
the pressure of work prevented her following up her
temptation that day, and slowly the vision faded.

Besides, Dai was very chatty that week, using Penny
to ease his conscience about the car loan. 'Leo is doing
his strong silent act,' he confessed one morning.

'I can't say I blame him.' But Penny wasn't in the
mood to make Dai feel any worse than he obviously did.
'Never mind—you must be able to repay soon.'

'Not this month, I'm afraid. But naturally, I'm taking
things easy now, spending nothing except petrol money
—but she is a thirsty lady, I must confess.' They were
leaving the surgery together. It was for once a sunny
morning. Penny had got used to the piles of litter in the
back alleys. The Aston was parked at the kerb, her silver
paint spotless, though her wheels couldn't but be

covered with the grime and filth of the gutter. Dai said, his voice warm with pride, 'She's a beauty, Penny—you can't deny it.'

'I don't blame you, Dai, I don't blame you a bit. She's your protection against the reality of all this.' Penny pointed to the mess, waiting for non-existent bin men or road sweepers. 'Perhaps everyone should have some bright spark—something that makes life beautiful. Even though you shouldn't have done it, I see why you did.'

Dai grinned. 'Hey, Penny, what's with the philosophising? The protection against reality? *She's* a reality. What's your protection, then, little Penny? What do you do about the bleakness of reality, then?'

'Get depressed.' But she said it with a brilliant smile.

But Dai was not as superficial as he pretended. 'You don't go out much, do you?'

'No. Too tired, really.'

'Would you like to go to a show? A night club? We do have them, you know.'

'Thanks for asking, but not at the moment. Maybe some other time.'

'No, I'm serious. You need cheering up.'

She gave him another smile. 'You have cheered me already by being so thoughtful—honestly. I'll call you if I need a shoulder to cry on.'

'Mind you do, girl.' Dai waved cheerfully, as he unlocked the door, got in, and zoomed down his electric window to wave again as he purred away from the grubby roadside. She watched him go. Lucky man, to have a toy he loved.

When Penny got back, it was later than she intended, as she had to go back to the surgery to look up some notes before admitting a child with asthma. So she wasn't surprised to see Leo's Rover parked outside Joanie's flat; he did sometimes pop in for a chat.

'Hello.' Leo and Joanie were sitting over the kitchen table. The table was strewn with bills—Penny saw that

they were headed with the same name as the letter from
Gemma's school.

'Hello, Penny,' smiled Joanie. 'I'll get your lunch.'

'No hurry if you're busy.'

Leo said, 'Not really busy, but worried. Joanie tells
me you know about Gemma's behaviour at school.'

'Yes.' As she spoke, Penny's mind began to work
overtime. Why was Leo so very concerned? Could those
bills be his? Was that why Joanie was unwilling to say
who was paying . . .

'I think your suggestion about a local school is a very
good one. It's not going to be easy, though. She's a
rather headstrong girl.'

'Don't worry, I'm a bit tough myself,' smiled Penny.

Leo looked up, and his frown cleared, the eyebrows
returning to their less severe position. 'Yes, I've
noticed.' For a moment they shared the joke. But then
her suspicions returned. Why was Leo sitting here,
concerned so seriously over Joanie's child? She turned
away. How old was Leo? He looked not more than
thirty-five; Joanie was forty if she was a day. And now
she looked much older, with the weight of worry on her
thin shoulders . . . Penny tried to tell herself that it was
no business of hers. Yet she felt hurt, to be left out. If
they wanted her help, it would be right to be frank with
her.

Leo's voice deepened. 'I'm very grateful. There's no
need for you to involve yourself——'

'Nonsense! I've a lot to thank Joanie for. I can't sit
around and see her miserable.' But she didn't want to
hang around with them; she felt rather like an outsider.
'I say, Joanie, I'll just have a bite to eat, and then take
Bathsheba for a run.'

But when she took the leash from its hook, and
Bathsheba had flung herself into her arms, Penny found
the tall frame of Leo Zander standing there. 'Mind if I
join you?' he asked.

'Of course not.' She was the one who had told him to take more exercise, after all. 'If you've finished the discussion.'

Joanie called from the kitchen, 'Yes, thanks. I don't know what I'd do without you two nice people. I feel much better about things now. Go and have a good walk. I'll have the kettle on when you get back.'

So they crossed the road, went down to the wide stretch of grass by the beach. The wind was wild, the breakers spectacular. They didn't speak much at first, enjoying the freshness, the sprightly antics of the dog, and the feeling of release from the tensions of the Gemma affair. Penny looked up at the silent figure of her employer. He was nice—still a bit of a cold efficient machine, but she felt safe with him, even proud to be in his company.

He caught her look. 'You were right, Doctor, I need more fresh air.'

She laughed. 'Well, that's one piece of advice that suits almost everyone. I wouldn't go far wrong with that.'

'You don't go far wrong with much, Penny. I wonder if you're getting used to Liverpool? Thinking that perhaps it wouldn't be the end of the world to stay?'

She tried to be honest. 'It isn't a bed of roses,' she admitted.

'I made that clear from the beginning.'

'You also made it clear you really wanted a man.'

He stopped walking. The wind blew his hair, making it informally casual, easing the severity of his appearance. 'Penny, I take that back. With all my heart I apologise for that. You're a welcome addition to our practice. You're good at your job. You've done a lot for us—I admit that freely, and gratefully.'

She said quickly, 'You've taught me a lot too. I feel as though I've grown up—and you've been a patient teacher.'

'I don't want to lose you, you know. The agreement was a six-month assistantship with a view to partnership.' He was outlined against a fitful sun. For that moment he had lost his autocratic look. He was a man, quite a handsome man, and his dark eyes were sincere as he offered her the chance of working with him for the rest of her working life. 'Penny, I hope you're going to give it a chance.'

She felt suddenly absurdly pleased. Leo had admitted he was wrong so openly—almost charmingly. She had never seen him so natural, so gentle, with anyone else. She tried to hide the burst of delight. 'I'll think it over. After all, I'm not getting any younger.'

Leo laughed. 'Oh, Penny, you must be at least twenty-five!'

'At least!' She made no admissions. 'The career structure isn't easy for women. But I'm determined to make it—and to give my fair share of loyalty and hard work —wherever I end up.'

'I know.' And the look from those dark eyes made her heart lurch suddenly in her chest. He was being so nice. When he was being nice, his face was as devastating as any film star. She found herself wondering what it would be like to be the centre and idol of those brooding eyes—and knew it would be like drowning in an ocean of warm, sensual security . . . She found herself blushing, and turned away to look for Bathsheba. Sensual was a word she had never imagined herself using for Leo Zander . . .

'You're feeling cold, Penny. Your cheeks are red.'

She pretended it was the wind. 'A little. But it's nice when you get home.'

'You're off duty on Wednesday?' asked Leo.

'Yes.'

'Any plans?'

'Relax and listen to music.'

'Come and listen to music at my place. Mrs Banks

does a casserole for us on a Wednesday, because she doesn't stay in the evening.'

'For "us"?' she queried.

'My father and I.'

'Of course—your father lives with you.'

'Yes. I'm told he should be in a home—and my answer is that he is.

'I see.'

Penny sat and thought about Leo Zander after he had driven away. For a man she had designated a cold fish, he was proving to have all kinds of humanity, all kinds of qualities. She knew he never complained about going out at night. She had seen his care and comfort to Joanie about Gemma. And now she had seen his quiet devotion to his father.

She had admired him at their first interview—as a man she could learn medicine from. But now she realised she could learn a great deal more. Her admiration had grown enormously since she had first known him. From finding him cold and unapproachable—now she wasn't sure. He had been open with her—yet she felt he was still holding back. She might admire him, but she felt she could never know him. She would never feel totally at ease with him, until she had discovered what it was he was keeping hidden from her—and from the world.

And as she stood at the door of his elegant white dormer bungalow on Sunset Strip the following Wednesday, wearing her best wool dress in dark green, she felt a trace of nervousness. She looked out, across the green grass where they had taken Bathsheba for a walk. There were hardy souls with their dogs in spite of the almost gale force winds that evening. But the sunset was gloriously magnificent, with dark purple clouds crossing the blaze of orange and magenta. The whole was reflected in the tossing waters of the Mersey estuary.

Penny sensed Leo's closeness. He had come out, and was standing beside her. 'Oh, I'm sorry——'

'No, Penny, keep looking. Have you ever seen such glory?'

She turned to look into his eyes. Instead of their usual darkness, she saw the sunset in them, reflected, and she felt suddenly that she knew what it was that Leo Zander was keeping a secret. It was his inner self.

'Come in. It's cold, and you can see the sunset just as well from the window.' The light had gone from his eyes, but she knew now that there could be passion there, and she wondered if she was supposed to know. Surely it was his secret? 'It's nice to see you.' His voice was gentle.

'For a moment I wondered if I had the wrong day,' Penny confessed.

'You wouldn't get that wrong. You're never wrong in such things, I've noticed.'

'You'll mention that in my reference when I leave?'

'Naturally. *If* you leave.' And he smiled with equanimity at her look. She smiled back; it was impossible not to.

And then she began to worry a little. It was always hard to say no to Leo. If he wanted her to stay, she might agree, against her better judgment. She must be wary of giving in to him. He would be better off with a man partner, a man who came from the city, who loved Liverpool and its people. And it's peculiarities. She would have learned a lot; but she would be glad to go.

The long lounge was discreetly lit. Penny had seen it before, when she came for drinks to meet the other partners. Tonight she had more time to appreciate the delicate good taste of the décor. 'Come, sit where you can see the changing tapestry of the sunset life.' Leo gestured her to the window seat. 'Dog-owners oblige me with a lot of fun. And that girl on the horse along the sands—don't you feel you could write a novel about her? Always alone, poor child.'

'Poor child?' she queried.

'Poor—in friends. She has that horse for company.'

He handed Penny a sherry. 'It's the same Fino that you drink.'

'Thank you.'

'Tell me about your life, Penny. What cities do you know, apart from Liverpool?'

'I've only lived in Brighton, where I was born, Oxford where I studied, then London and Banbury,' she told him.

'Haven't you found that you get used to where you are—come to appreciate it?'

Penny smiled. She held up her glass to him. 'Don't make me admit any more! I and your city are incompatible. Here's to a truce on this topic.'

Leo lifted his glass. 'Agreed. Sorry to be a bore, Penny. Perhaps you can teach me how to be livelier?'

'I'm not lively, am I?'

'Natural,' he smiled. 'I'm beginning to be afraid when you decide to speak your mind.'

'I don't believe that for one minute. You're afraid of nothing.'

'Not quite true.' Leo was standing by her, as they both looked out at the setting sun. Penny felt a shiver of anticipation, as though he were going to admit what frightened him. She was conscious of the warmth of his body, the smell of his suit, and the trace of aftershave from his sleeked-back hair.

At that moment there was a high-pitched buzz. He said, 'That's the oven bell. The casserole is done, and I must go and give Father his meal. Would you care to meet him? He's watching television in the other room —he won't be joining us for supper.'

There was a savoury smell issuing from the direction of the kitchen, and Penny began to feel quite hungry. She followed Leo into the television room, where a small white-haired man with a white beard was sitting curled up in a wheelchair, staring at the television screen with blank eyes. 'Hello, Father. This is Penny, my partner.'

The old man held out his hand in what seemed to be a reflex action. 'How do you do?'

But his eyes were still blank. Penny said, 'Good evening, Dr Zander.'

Leo murmured, 'My dear, his eating is a little erratic. If you would be kind enough to go through to my music centre, and choose some tapes for us to listen to over supper, I'll give Father his meal, and join you in a few moments.'

She saw that he preferred it, and agreed to leave them for a while. She began to sort through his library of tapes and records. But her attention was more on the man she had just left—the dedicated man who put duty first in his life. What was it he was frightened of? Was it growing old and lonely like his father? With no family to care for him? In spite of his elegant home, his prestige in the community, his wealth, Penny felt sorry for Leo. His patients were his only family; the only human warmth in his life came from their gratitude.

At that moment, there was a loud knock at the back door, and Penny heard Leo answer it. She heard a woman's voice, loud and rather plummy. She heard them chatting together, then the door was opened into the lounge. 'Penny, my dear, this is my next-door neighbour, Janet Rhys-Evans. This is my junior partner, Janet—Penny Harcourt.'

The woman who came in brought with her the whiff of expensive perfume. She was buxom but stately, her dark hair dramatic with a silver streak at one side. Her dark dress was well tailored and chic, and she wore patent leather shoes that must have cost three figures.

Penny smiled at her with her natural pleasantness. Naturally in this part of town one would expect to meet wealthy people. She noticed the dark eyes of Mrs Rhys-Evans search her own modest dress, identify her shoes as from Marks & Spencers. 'How nice to meet you.' They shook hands. Mrs Rhys-Evans continued,

'You look terribly young, Penny. Are you really a doctor?'

The old story. Penny took it well. 'Oh yes, really a doctor. You should see my college friend. She's a gynaecologist at the Royal Free, and she's five feet high. But once you've seen her grappling with breech twins, you realise that appearances can be deceptive.'

The elegant neighbour looked slightly alarmed. 'I'll take your word for it!'

'If you would excuse me for a moment, I'll just see to Father.' Leo left them together, after refusing any help as both women offered.

Janet helped herself to sherry, and sat down in a most familiar way. 'I pop in most evenings,' she explained. 'Mrs Banks is here, but I think they're glad of some help with Dr Lionel. I'm a widow, with time on my hands. Leo and I are very close—very close indeed.'

Penny felt this was a message to her to stay out of Leo's affairs. She sensed rather than heard jealousy in the older woman's voice. It amused her to think she might be thought a rival for Leo's affections. 'I'm only here for six months.' She smiled to herself as she saw relief in the other woman's eyes; she could scarcely be called a rival. In that case, 'I just came round to see some of Leo's music,' she explained.

'You like music? Let me put something on for you.' Janet was quick to demonstrate her skill with the music centre. 'We often spend hours just listening. The heavy stuff is in this cupboard, this is Strauss and Sullivan, and there are some modern symphonies on this shelf.'

'I'll leave it to you to choose.'

The arrival of Janet Rhys-Evans had somehow spoiled the evening, even when Leo came back. Janet showed no sign of going—and Leo showed no sign of inviting her to join them. So she stayed, drinking sherry and making small talk, until it was clear by the smell that the casserole was rather spoilt. Even in her annoyance,

Penny felt a bit sorry for Janet. It couldn't be much fun being a widow. She must long for conversation. And quite possibly she hoped for more from Leo. A single man next door must be a widow's dream—especially a handsome one. Penny smiled to herself, and forgave Janet for making the casserole leathery.

It was after nine when Janet went, after telling Penny in detail all the different charities she was chairman of, and how much in demand she was at lunches. Leo came back after seeing her off. He opened his mouth to try to apologise, but saw the twinkle in Penny's eye and they both laughed. 'The dinner will be ruined. But Janet comes quite a lot. I wanted to show her that she isn't the boss here—yet.'

Penny wasn't sure what to make of that, but she said, 'Never mind. I've learned an awful lot about how the other half live.'

'She's very sweet to Father,' Leo put in.

'You were very sweet to her. I'm glad you didn't tell her to go.'

'I like Janet.' He was enigmatic now. 'Shall we see what dire fate has overtaken our chicken casserole?'

He opened a bottle of wine, and insisted Penny sip it while he prepared the meal. 'You may not notice the faults after some wine,' he explained.

And the meal was merrier than she could have imagined. Leo was witty but a good host. The chicken was a bit dry, but delicious nonetheless. And as they took coffee through to the lounge, Penny felt truly happy and relaxed. They had managed to spend the entire evening together without any disagreement. All the same, she felt as though she knew Leo only a little better. She knew more about his kindness, and his humanity. But she knew none of his secrets, and very little about his real feelings.

'Have some Benedictine with your second cup?' The fresh coffee fragrance filled the room.

Penny looked up with alarm. 'Leo, look at the time! We have to work tomorrow.'

'You're right. Next time we'll make it a Saturday.'

Next time. That was nice, Leo assuming she would be coming again, even with a widow lurking in the background.

At the door, she turned to thank him, but he accompanied her to her car. 'Take care, Penny,' he told her.

'I will,' she smiled. 'It's been a lovely evening. I'm grateful.'

He smiled back. 'You noticed that I obeyed you—I never spoke of the subject you tabooed.'

'That was nice of you.'

'I can be nice sometimes,' he assured her.

There was something touching about that, and she looked up at him with a little frown. 'Oh, Leo, of course you can!' And as she looked up, he bent down and gently touched her lips with his. It was a mere whisper of a kiss, but its effect was more electric than Penny could have imagined. She got hastily into the car, murmured her thanks, and drove away. But her heart was racing as she drove along the silent streets, her whole being alive and trembling with a feeling so sweet that she didn't recognise it.

CHAPTER FIVE

GEMMA FAIRBROTHER was due home at the end of the following week, and Joanie was becoming increasingly agitated at the idea. Penny had thought that she and Leo between them had calmed Joanie down, but as the days went on, it was clear that she was very apprehensive.

'Oh, Penny,' she moaned, 'why don't they give classes in being a parent? I'm so totally useless at it. Fancy being terrified of your own kid! That can't be right.'

Penny opened her little black bag. 'I don't believe in handing out tranquillisers, Joanie, but I think perhaps you'd better take one of these at night—at least you'll sleep better. And don't forget your prayers, Joanie.' She had not seen Joanie go to church, but a touch of Robin White's remedy couldn't harm. 'Then you know you aren't alone—not ever.'

Joanie's pale face brightened when she smiled. 'Penny Harcourt, you're such a nice person. Thank the Lord I listened to Leo when he told me I ought to have a lodger!'

Penny smiled too. 'Leo's a great fixer. He seems to have his finger in all sorts of pies.' She waited for more confessions about Leo, but Joanie made no sign. Penny shook her head. What was Leo's interest in Gemma? Surely it was more than that of a good and supportive family doctor? She sensed that there was more to it than met the eye, yet neither Joanie nor Leo came close to admitting anything.

Gemma was due to arrive the following evening. Penny would be at surgery, and Gemma would be there when she got back. She was curious to meet the girl, to get to know her, and to see how mother and daughter really got on. She ascended the steps, making no attempt to keep quiet, and let herself in, calling, 'Hello, Joanie, I'm back!'

Through the door, she heard a muffled sob. She hesitated; it was hard to know what to do. 'Are you all right?' she asked.

The door was pulled violently open. 'No, she's not all right. She wasn't there to meet me. And I had to go through her bag to find the cab fare.' The girl who stood there was white-faced and untidy, her hair spiked up in points, her limbs ungainly and her eyes unhappy and hard. She wore a long straight skirt that emphasised the thinness. She said in a high, tense voice, 'If you're any good as a doctor you'd better tell me what's up with her.'

'Oh no!' Joanie was slumped on the sofa, her eyes blinking and unseeing. Penny was at her side in a moment. 'Joanie, Joanie, wake up!' She shook her fiercely. 'What have you taken? Gemma, I think it might be the tranquillisers. Phone for the ambulance—the number is on the wall by the phone.'

'An ambulance?' The girl's resentful attitude vanished, leaving a small and frightened child. 'Oh, Mum!' But she went and obeyed Penny, who tried to rouse Joanie to a sitting position. As Penny worked, she heard the child's whimpers, like a frightened puppy, but she had to give Joanie all her attention.

'Gemma, will you phone Uncle Leo, please. Do you know his number?'

'Yes.' Still scared, Gemma obeyed, seemingly relieved to have an adult taking charge. She ran to the phone. Leo was there in minutes, but Joanie would not come round.

'Ambulance?' They had heard the siren, and Leo went to the door. 'In here.' They lifted the limp form on to a stretcher. 'I'll follow in my car,' Leo muttered to Penny. 'Stay with Gemma. I'll phone as soon as there's anything to report.' At the door he turned again. 'Have you any idea what it might be?'

'Only Valium. I gave her some to take at night, just this week.' Penny shook her head. She couldn't believe that someone as down-to-earth as Joanie Fairbrother could do such a thing. Of course she was nervous, but not when she knew it would affect Gemma just about as badly as anything else. She put her hand on the girl's thin shoulder as the stretcher was taken down to the waiting ambulance. The siren sounded again, and they saw the lights flashing bright blue through the front window. Gemma's face was tragic.

'Don't worry,' Penny reassured her. 'She'll be all right.' There weren't enough tablets for the dose to be fatal.

'I'm not worried.' Gemma shook Penny's hand from her shoulder and went to sit on the sofa, stroking Bathsheba, who was walking round, knowing something was wrong. The bitch settled by Gemma, and she stroked the sleek head hard, her pale face set, her eyes tearless. 'An overdose, wasn't it?'

Penny said quickly, 'We don't know yet.'

'Oh yes, we do. It's obvious.'

'Gemma, it isn't your fault,' urged Penny.

'Who said it was?' Gemma snapped the words, and stroked the dog more fiercely.

Penny stood up. 'I'll make some toast. Do you want some?'

'No.'

Penny said nothing else. She went to the kitchen and warmed some tomato soup. She made some buttered toast, laid two places at the kitchen table, and made a pot of tea. She was relieved that Gemma's temper didn't affect her sense of smell. She must have been starving, and the smell of buttered toast got through where words would have had no effect. They sat and ate silently, waiting for the phone to ring.

Penny washed the dishes and left them to drain. 'I'll be in my room if you want me, Gemma,' she said.

'I won't.' But as though the words were torn from her, Gemma said, 'She will be all right? You did say? You are a doctor, aren't you?'

'Yes. But they'll keep her in for observation, I think. She should be back tomorrow.' Penny's voice was cool; she knew any fuss would freeze the child away again.

'You some sort of friend of hers?'

'Yes, you could say that.'

'Uncle Leo'll be worried,' said Gemma.

'I know. But he knows I'll look after you.'

'You look like a schoolgirl yourself.' Gemma was scornful. Then incidentally she said, 'Our prefects are scum.'

'Well, I'm not, and you'd better believe it.'

Gemma looked up at the unaccustomed sharpness of Penny's reply. She looked down again, but there was a look of more respect in her sad eyes. Penny felt desperately sorry for her. The diagnosis had been right: The child was lonely for love, and wanted to come home. What damage this episode might have, Penny tried not to think. She wondered if it was too soon to mention school; it might make things easier for Joanie.

'Would you like to go to Merchants instead of Francis Smythe?' she asked. 'Your mum and your uncle were going to ask you.'

'What for?' But there was a diffident interest in the set of Gemma's determined little jaw.

'I think you know.'

'You mean that lousy Miss Dartford wrote to Mum? She said she didn't want me around, but I don't care what she says—or does. I don't give a damn where I go. I won't stay anywhere any longer than I have to, I tell you that!'

Penny looked around the homely little room, bereft of its owner. Poor child, to come home to this. She went round putting the small lamps on, drawing the curtains on the lighted container terminal in the distance. 'I don't think this was a deliberate overdose. Joanie hasn't been sleeping well. I think she may have taken one or two tablets in the night, and then forgot, and took a couple more this morning. She was excited at you coming—she was looking forward to it. She was going to make a cake.'

'Like hell she was!' But the girl's anger was low and sullen now. 'She was only cheerful on the days she took me back to the station.'

Penny said, 'That's why she wants you to go to Merchants.' The girl said nothing, and Penny went on, 'I hated my school too.'

'Boarding school?' Penny nodded. 'I bet it wasn't as lousy as mine.'

'It wasn't lousy at all. But if you don't like something, then you call it names, I suppose.'

'You're only saying that to make me feel better. I bet you never got into trouble. I bet you were a little goody-goody—a teachers' pet.'

Penny allowed herself to smile. 'You're quite bright for a brat. You can see through me. But it's true I was miserable every start of term.' She stood up. 'I wonder if your mother did make that cake.' She walked into the kitchen, trying to forget that they were waiting for the phone to ring, that every minute that passed without Leo phoning meant that Joanie wasn't settled for the night. As she lifted a pile of tins, she saw that Gemma was standing beside her. 'Which tin might it be in?' she asked.

The girl picked up one. 'This.' She shook it, and the sound of something solid came from it. 'This lid is the tightest.' She opened it, and tipped out a rather well-done sponge. 'Shall we have some?'

Penny had never felt less like a slice of burnt sponge cake, but she agreed; it would pass the time. Gemma cut two generous slices. 'Funny how she could make a cake if she took all those pills.' Gemma had already bitten into her slice, and spoke with her mouth full.

'Even if she felt funny, she wanted to do it for you, you see,' Penny told her. Gemma took another bite, while Penny nibbled a small piece. 'Why don't you have a nice hot bath, and get ready for bed?'

'I don't feel like it.' But Gemma looked keenly at Penny, who pretended to enjoy her cake, and didn't care whether Gemma bathed or not. 'Oh, all right, I might as well. Come to the bathroom, Bathsheba, then I can splash you.'

Penny didn't turn a hair. 'I'll make another cup of tea when you've finished.' She ignored the threat of splashing. She had established a link with Gemma, fragile though it was. She wasn't a bad kid at all. She heard her run the bath, then turn her transistor radio on rather loud. She ignored that too—just for tonight. After all, there was only the empty dental lab downstairs.

Suddenly Penny heard a key in the door. Leo? She stood up, but she didn't want to alarm Gemma, so she walked quietly to the hall. Leo was coming in, his arm around Joanie's waist. She was upright, and her eyes were less blank. 'Oh, Joanie—thank goodness!' Penny went to meet her, and helped her to a chair.

Leo stood looking down at her. 'All right now?'

'Yes, thank you.'

'You promise this is the last time?'

'Yes, I do, Leo—very faithfully.'

'Shall I tell Penny?' he asked her.

'Yes.'

'It was a hangover, Penny.' Leo's voice was displeased, but resigned. 'She helped herself to half a bottle of vodka at lunchtime.'

Penny said quietly, 'Was the fear that bad, Joanie? The kettle is on, and Gemma is in the bath, if you hadn't realised by now.'

'I was very silly,' Joanie admitted. 'I'd taken the tablets you gave me as well, and I didn't realise the effect at first—only when I stood up.'

Penny said briskly, 'Well, you've had a bad lesson. Do you want some tea, or just to go to bed?'

'Bed. But I'll just say hello to Gemma.' Joanie's face showed regret—and determination like that Penny had seen in her daughter earlier. She stood up unaided, and went to the bathroom. 'Gemma, I'm back, love, and I'm just off to bed. Sleep well.'

Penny smiled at Leo, when Gemma gave a little shout of surprise. 'Okay. See you tomorrow. The cake wasn't all that soft, but we ate it.'

And Joanie managed a smile as she went to her own room. Leo said, 'Well, I'd better let you get to bed too.' He went to the door. 'Are you invited to Chris Santani's tomorrow?'

'Yes, but I'm on call.'

'You should go. Lalla is an excellent cook.'

'Maybe. I'll see how things are here,' Penny told him.

'I think those two should be left alone to sort things out. You have your work to think of.' He smiled. 'Well, we seem to have our crises, don't we, Penny? Thank goodness this one was a small one.'

She watched him go. It was a puzzle. Somehow this family meant a great deal to him; but no one wanted to talk about it. Secrets, secrets . . . But tonight she was too tired to worry about it.

It was Saturday. They all got up late. Penny heard the murmurs of voices—friendly enough voices. Joanie and Gemma were getting on without any tantrums. Penny had to wait for the bathroom, and she realised that if Gemma had come home for good, Joanie would need her spare rooms. Penny must look for other accommodation for the rest of her short time in Liverpool.

She went to morning surgery, glad it was quiet, as she

was on her own on Saturday. She was just writing down her list of calls afterwards when Kay came in to say that there was a call from Lalla Santani, Chris's wife. 'It's about tonight,' she added.

'Thanks, Kay.' Penny picked up the phone. 'Hello, Lalla.'

'Good morning. I just wanted to remind you that we are expecting you this evening. You might have forgotten to put our telephone number on the answering machine.' Lalla's English was good, and she spoke precisely, with the careful enunciation of the Indian.

Penny had hoped to escape with the excuse that she was too busy tonight, but it was difficult to refuse, with her charming hostess on the line. 'It's good of you to ask me—and for reminding me. I'll leave the message that I'm at your number until midnight, then. And thank you again.'

She had met Lalla Santani once before. She was quiet, but very friendly and hospitable, and she made it clear that she found life in Britain very wearing. 'We had servants in India,' she had confided. 'When my children were naughty, I could go away and leave them. But now it is all work, work, work. I am so glad I have only two children. I must do everything myself, and it is not easy for me.'

'You could advertise for some help with the house-work,' Penny suggested.

'My husband will not hear of it. He tells me that I am alone in the house all day, and that I have nothing else to do but keep it beautiful.' Lalla took without question that her husband's wishes must be obeyed. Penny said nothing; it was Lalla's own affair. But she could see how undisciplined the children were—a girl of nearly three, and a little boy of one. They ran free in the house, and demanded to be the centre of attention whenever there were any visitors. Lalla was a pretty woman, but her large black eyes were ringed with the grey of weariness.

Penny dressed carefully that evening. Joanie and Gemma had been shopping together in town, and were happily discussing clothes and shoes. It would have been pleasant to sit at home with them, but she knew she must make an attempt to be sociable. The Santanis were so kind to invite her.

But even her best navy silk dress looked drab when she arrived. The hall was full of people, spilling out from the lounge and on to the stairs, chatting mostly in Hindi. The women looked magnificent, in vivid colours, the silks and chiffons trimmed with gold and silver, handsome necks swathed in gold chains, wrists jangling with bangles set with diamonds. Penny stood, overwhelmed, and slipped off her grey flannel jacket, feeling like a pauper in her best party dress, with Auntie Hilda's simple gold locket round her neck. Her hair, too—shampooed or not, there was little she could do with her dark hair except brush it back. Here there were elaborate chignons trimmed with flowers, with jewels and glittering ornaments among glossy black curls and ringlets.

She asked for orange juice because she was on call. But as she was introduced to some of the glittering company, she noticed that all the women drank only soft drinks, and was glad that she had at least not made the mistake of asking for anything stronger.

'You look very charming, Dr Harcourt,' Lalla Santani told her.

'Thank you. Please call me Penny.'

The conversation was hard to follow because it slipped from English to Hindi and back again without the ladies noticing. Most of them were doctors' wives and much of their talk was about their homes, which sounded very luxurious indeed. Penny brightened up for a moment when she saw Dai arrive with his girl-friend of the moment, a nurse called Andrea. But Andrea must have been to the Santanis' before, and she was wearing a low-cut dress in royal blue, trimmed with sequins, and looked as gorgeous as the Indians.

Some of the women drifted into the kitchen, where the most delicious mixture of smells rose from the dishes on the stove. Lalla looked splendid in glossy dark green silk edged with gold. Her hair was tied back with a gold ribbon, and flowed down past her waist. 'Come and look, Penny. You like Indian food, I hope?'

'Oh yes, thank you.'

'I enjoy cooking very much. And because many of my guests have brought their children, my own are not bothering me tonight, so I enjoy very much.' Penny could hear the bumps and squeals from upstairs. But Chris had put some haunting Indian music on the stereo, which hid the children's worst gambols.

At that moment, above the noise, the telephone rang. 'Who's on call?' shouted Chris; in a houseful of doctors, there were several. Penny raised her hand too, and edged towards the phone. 'Yes, I'll get her.' Chris beckoned Penny. 'It's the Williams boy.'

Penny covered one ear, so that she could hear with the other. 'Yes?'

'Doctor, I'm sorry—Steve here. It's Gordon. He sort of passed out.'

'What's he doing now?' she asked.

'Just sitting down. He went all funny, and pale. He says he feels tired and wants to go to bed.'

'Let him go to bed. But I'll come round.' It could be nothing, but she had better make sure. No abnormality had been found in any of his tests, so it was possibly psychological. But Penny couldn't afford to take a chance.

'But we are just serving the food,' Chris protested.

'You could have something to eat first.'

'It's only a faint, Penny.' Chris was sure.

'I'd better see him,' Penny said firmly. 'He's been worrying me.'

'Don't forget to come back. You mustn't go without eating.'

'All right.' She made her escape, though by that time she was feeling quite hungry, and looking forward to the fluffy rice and curries that were just then being put out on the crisp starched tablecloth.

She smiled to herself as she looked down at the dark dress. She would have felt silly now in chiffon and jewels. She got into the car and headed for Bootle. It was dark, with no moon, and the wind was chilly but not too strong.

Gordon was not in bed, but sitting in a chair, his face tense and white. 'I don't know what happened,' he told her. But he obviously felt scared about it.

Stephen said, 'He just slipped on to the floor and twitched his arms a bit.'

'For how long?' Penny took out her sphygmomano-meter.

'Only a minute or two. But it seemed like ages.' Stephen looked worried too. 'What do you think it was?'

'I don't know exactly,' said Penny, 'but I know that I don't think your depression is all in the mind any more. I want you to go to the neurology department at the hospital. I'd like their opinion.'

'Tonight?'

'Yes, tonight, Steve. Can you get his pyjamas and a toothbrush? I'll give the registrar a ring.'

She arranged admission without any trouble. 'Don't worry, boys,' she told them. 'It's only the best neuro department in the North of England.'

Gordon managed a smile at that. 'You know, Dr Harcourt, that's the first time I've heard you praise Liverpool!'

'Maybe I'm getting to know it better,' she smiled.

'You should. We're not all bad, you know. In our street, the folk'll do anything for you. They were great with me mum. They've got good hearts here, Doctor, and that's important. She used to say that.' Gordon's voice tailed off.

'I agree with you.' Penny waited until the ambulance came, then she drove away, feeling very sorry for Kevin and Stephen. Some families just seemed to have bad luck. She had long ago stopped wondering why it always seemed to be the good ones . . .

Her spirits lifted as she drove into the Santanis' elegant driveway and saw that Leo's Rover was there. It would be nice to discuss the case with him. She locked the car and walked up to the door with optimism, a smile already on her lips. She saw Chris through the frosted glass, coming to let her in.

'Come in, Penny. There's lots left.' Chris handed her a glass of wine. But Penny's eyes had gone straight to a familiar figure in the hall, a large woman in purple velvet, with dripping diamonds in her ears, and her white streak showing up beautifully in her upswept dark hair. It was Janet Rhys-Evans.

Janet greeted her warmly. 'Do come through. The curry is magnificent!'

Lalla was in the dining room, talking to Leo. Penny helped herself to food, but her appetite had diminished. She put it down to worry about Gordon—yet why worry when he was in good hands?

Chris was a good host. 'How was the Williams boy?' he wanted to know.

'I had to admit him,' Penny told him. 'But it was useful my being on call, because I knew the family history.'

Chris had the warmth of several glasses of wine in his voice as he said, 'That is what is nice about our practice —the families become your family.'

She smiled into his darkly handsome face. His eyes were liquidly gentle, his expression admiring. She said, 'I'm beginning to see that.'

He put one arm around her shoulders to steer her

towards the table. 'Come, you must try this pickle.' He did not remove his arm. 'Yes, our patients are our children. For me it took longer to realise this, because I did not regard the people as my people. But I do now. Their affection is not easy to gain, but when you have it, it is worth having, Penny.' And he squeezed her warmly, his breath on her hair. She began to feel slightly uncomfortable.

'I'd better say hello to Leo,' she said.

He let go reluctantly. 'We must talk more. Perhaps I can help you to settle down? The patients speak of you with respect already. Soon it will be affection also.' He gazed into her eyes again. He had beautiful eyes, blacker than Leo's but not so deeply unreadable. Penny was relieved when his wife called him to pass round more wine.

But when she looked around for Leo he was deep in conversation with Janet, so she backed away, and talked to a lively little Indian lady instead. She felt let down, somehow. She had been looking forward to a chat with Leo. Somehow his words were solid and worth hearing; they gave stability to her own when he agreed with her. She smiled at him over Janet's shoulder, and he edged towards her, but Janet came with him.

After a little small talk, Leo asked, 'Is Gemma all right?'

'I believe she is.' Penny put down her empty glass. 'But she does take a long time in the bathroom. I shall have to look for another place to live.'

'Not yet, surely? She's going back to school until Christmas. The other Head won't take her in mid-term.'

'That gives me time to look out.'

Janet said, 'I'll keep my ears open, dear. It's just for a few weeks, isn't it?'

'Yes—November, December, January and half of February.'

'Only four months.' Leo said the words, but it was very difficult to tell what was in his voice—was he teasing or pleading? 'No, surely you won't leave till Christmas. That only leaves January and February. Hardly worth bothering to move.'

'Perhaps. I can always have my baths in the middle of the night.' Penny made light of it. Janet was clearly glad the time was so short. She still treated Leo as her property, warned Penny off with as many signals as she could without actually putting it into words. Penny was glad it was time to leave.

Next day was Sunday and she had no calls at all. It was wonderful just to lie on the sofa in her own room, and relax completely. Jade, the black cat, had taken a fancy to Penny's room, and curled up beside her with a condescending friendliness. The warmth of the furry bundle was better than a hot water bottle. Winter was drawing in, and the air outside was chill, the sky white and cold, the branches dark against it, the river steely grey.

Penny heard the doorbell, and a spark of hope came that it was Leo; he certainly treated this family as his own, when it came to popping in. But when the knock came to her own door, it was Chris Santani's dark face that looked round it. 'May I come in, Penny? You are not busy?'

'Far from it.' She sat up and smoothed down her skirt. 'Come and sit down, Chris. What can I do for you?'

'The question is mine. I wanted to talk more last night, but as host I could not. You ought not to run away from our practice, Penny. You fit in well.'

'I'm not cut out for deprived areas. I lack sympathy with litter louts,' she told him.

'And is that all?' He had sunk on to the sofa beside her. 'Can you imagine my culture shock? The village where my parents live is so peaceful, bright and calm.

There are no pressures. The chickens run about in the yard, the vegetables and rice grow plentifully in the fields. Life is sweet there. Yet I must stay here. My children must be educated. Their future matters more than my happiness.'

Penny smiled. 'You wouldn't be happy in a village, Chris, not now. You love your BMW and your sports car, and I know Lalla loves her dishwasher. You'd get bored.'

He smiled. She admired the smoothness of his olive skin, the white perfection of his teeth, the kindness in his eyes. He moved a little nearer to her, and his hand moved behind her on the sofa back. 'You are perceptive as well as beautiful.'

'Neither, Chris. Don't flatter!'

'My wife never speaks so wisely. Mostly she moans —about the weather, about the children, about how hard she must work.'

'That's private between you and her,' Penny said firmly.

'Between us?' His voice was harsh suddenly. 'Between us is a great emptiness.' He looked down, and she felt a wave of sympathy. It must be hard for him. His job was taxing—and to come home to no support from his family must be hard. He could only confide in his colleagues—and she was a colleague.

'Let me get you a sherry,' she offered. 'Or tea?'

'Sherry, please.' He accepted a large one, drank it quickly, and asked politely for more. Penny sipped hers after refilling his glass.

Chris put down the empty glass. 'You are an understanding friend. Thank you.' And gently he squeezed her shoulders as he had done last night. Then before she realised what was happening, he bent and kissed her cheek. 'Thank you.' He kissed her again, and then before she could move away, put a stop to this embarrassing situation, he had kissed her full on the mouth—hard, but very quick. 'Forgive me—I must go.' And before she could think of a reply, he was gone.

CHAPTER SIX

On careful thought, Penny found it fairly easy to forgive Chris that impulsive kiss. He had already told her how his wife was unsympathetic. She had no personal knowledge of men—but she had read a great deal, and was well aware that Chris must be feeling sexually frustrated. His action had not been planned. He had been silly, but it was over, and she would make no judgment. They were colleagues, and must remain so for the next few weeks. She resolved to say nothing more about the incident, even though it unsettled her. She was a doctor, and surely capable of understanding a momentary aberration.

Fortunately she was kept extremely busy. The surgeries were crowded every day, and she had her regulars to see. Poor Gordon's skull scan had shown that he needed urgent brain surgery, and she had to go to tell the other brothers. She went one evening. The nights got very dark now, but she was used to the area. She knew to look out for debris in the road, for frightened cats, and for neglected children still playing with broken prams, or stealing older children's cigarettes while their parents played Bingo, or went to clubs.

Stephen and Kevin were subdued. They had been to see Gordon in hospital. 'He's fine. Nothing wrong with him,' they told her.

'Good. I came round in case there was anything you wanted to ask me,' said Penny.

'Tell us straight, Dr Harcourt.' Stephen stood up, prepared for the worst.

'Stephen, I'm not hiding anything. He has to have an operation, to repair a blood vessel inside the skull. But the surgeon is top class. He does this sort of operation all the time. I'm confident all will be well.'

'Inside his head?' Kevin shook his head firmly. 'You can't pretend that's not risky, Doctor. It's major surgery, isn't it?'

'Of course. But the surgeon will talk to you before the op. He has to do more tests, but he'll be frank with you, don't worry. And he'll answer any questions you have.'

The lads said they were satisfied, but there was apprehension in their eyes as Penny left them, to go to her car at the kerb. A jogger came hurtling round the corner, and almost knocked her over. 'I'm terribly sorry!' he exclaimed.

She knew that polite voice; it wasn't a Liverpool voice. 'Robin?'

He paused, and came back. 'Penny? How are you?' He seemed pleased.

'Fine. I see you're keeping fit.'

'And doing a few visits at the same time. Getting used to Liverpool, then?'

'Too busy to think about it,' she smiled.

'Too busy to stop for a drink?'

'No.'

'My, that was quick!' he laughed. 'I like a woman who makes up her mind.'

'Selfish of me, but I think I need a touch of your philosophy just now. You always put me in a better frame of mind.' Penny locked the car, and they crossed the road together to the Liverpool Arms. 'I've just been to see the Williams boys,' she told him. 'It wasn't easy.'

'It's been a bad year for them. Gordon has a tumour?'

'An aneurysm. He should make a complete recovery —but his brothers don't think so, poor souls.'

'Souls is my province,' said Robin. 'I'll call and chat. Reinforce the faith and hope bit. Half of bitter?'

'Please.'

As always, their conversation flowed easily, as though

they had been friends for years. Penny found she was confiding perhaps too much. She had mentioned Gemma, without realising that Robin knew nothing about her. 'I must stop using you as a—as a——' she began.

'No, Penny, it's all right. Let me help.'

She could have kissed him, he was so honest, so sincere. 'It isn't fair to you. Only—even Dr Santani has been—on my mind lately. I wish things would go smoothly—just for a day or two . . .'

'My dear girl, what a wish! You should just wish—or pray—for the strength to do the right thing. If you do that, what more can life expect of you?'

'That's very true. Robin, I wish I could put you in my pocket sometimes.'

He smiled, and the smile lit up those eyes as they looked into hers. Penny felt the load of the day lift from her shoulders as she smiled back.

She drove home refreshed. Robin White was good news. As she pushed open the door, Gemma came hurrying to meet her. 'Penny, Penny, you've just missed Leo!'

'Oh, shucks, fancy missing Leo,' joked Penny. 'Gemma dear, I've only worked with him all day, and I'm pretty sure I'll work with him tomorrow. Why does it matter that I missed him tonight?'

'Because—' Gemma was conspiratorial, 'because he came to ask us to go out for the day, to his boat in the Lake District. That's why.'

'How lovely!' Penny wasn't sure if 'we' meant her as well. 'I didn't know he had a boat.'

'It's my last weekend before I go back to Wormwood Scrubs——'

Joanie remonstrated, 'Come on, love, it's only for half a term!'

'Hooray! You're coming home!' Penny was encouraging.

'Not till Christmas. It's going to drag like anything.' Gemma had almost lost her petulant expression, since being home. 'Penny, do say you'll come
with us! Leo said to be sure to ask you, and let him
know.'

Joanie said, 'That's true. It's a picnic of sorts—we've
been before. He has a sailing dinghy on Derwentwater.
It's great fun, honestly—if the weather's good.'

Leo arrived for them early on Sunday morning. 'It's
very nice of you to include me,' said Penny quietly, as
they waited for Joanie and Gemma to bring the picnic
basket.

'Nonsense! You're part of the establishment. It
wouldn't be the same without you.' He was wearing a
pale blue sweater and jeans. It was amazing how much
more human he looked in casual clothes. The sky was
blue, though there was a cold wind. 'Have you never
seen Derwentwater?'

'Never.'

'I'm glad. I love watching people's faces when they see
it for the first time. It's magic.' The others joined them.
'Come on, let's not waste any sailing time.'

'Can I go in the front?' asked Gemma.

'All right, Gemma. Fasten the safety-belt.'

Leo drove well, but fast. His expensive engine purred
happily as they shot up the motorway, turning off to take
a more leisurely route through the Lyth Valley, where
the road wound and curled alongside the small rippling
river, and the hedgerows and trees were glorious in gold,
russet and scarlet autumn colours. The hazy October
sunshine lit them like a stage set, and the distant hills
were purple with heather, and orange with glowing
bracken.

Penny didn't speak much, so surprised and overcome
was she with the sudden blaze of beauty all about
her. But Gemma made up for it. She chattered to Leo
almost non-stop, explaining how some of the places in

Worcestershire—where her school was—were almost as lovely as this, but not quite.

He teased her gently, 'So Francis Smythe wasn't all bad?'

'No,' she shot an uncertain look at her mother, 'I didn't mind some of it.'

'But you're happy at coming home for good?'

'Oh yes, definitely! I've got to see the editor of the *Herald*, to ask if he'll take me on as a junior reporter.'

'*What?*' Joanie's voice rose. 'A reporter? They earn peanuts these days. It's a dead-end job, Gemma. You must go to university before you think of anything else these days.' Penny groaned inside herself. It had taken hours of quiet discussion with Gemma to find out what she really wanted to do—and Joanie had hit it all on the head.

But Leo, as usual, came to the rescue. 'We'll have lots of time to discuss Gemma's future. Let's see what exam results she gets at Merchants. Women do very well in reporting, Joanie. And judging by today, your daughter's certainly got the gift of the gab! It might be just the thing for her, who knows?'

'It is, Uncle Leo—I know it is.' Gemma was quick to enlist his support. 'Oh, look, there's the lake! Look, Penny—isn't it beautiful?'

It was. Penny almost held her breath as they drove along the edge of the gentle waters. 'To think this is only two hours away from Dourton!' she breathed. Leo turned round and smiled at her, before negotiating the next bend, where a gracious grey stone house stood in its own gardens, the lawn going right down to the lake. 'Is this yours? I can't believe it.'

'Not all of it, I'm afraid,' he told her. 'It's divided into flats. We have the bottom left-hand corner.' He pointed to the lake. 'And that's my little boat. I phoned and asked Jack to get her out for me.'

'Let's sail, let's sail!' Gemma was out of the car as soon

as Leo had pulled up. 'Look, Uncle Leo, the wind is just right!'

'I couldn't sail. I'm weak for lack of food,' he protested. 'Let's eat first—and drink. I've brought a bottle of Entre Deux Mers.'

'That means "Between two Seas"—daft name for wine. I don't suppose I'm allowed any,' complained Gemma.

'Of course you are.' Leo spoke quietly. 'You're grown up now.' And Penny smiled to herself, as she saw how the compliment made Gemma straighten her shoulders and look pleased. Leo was terribly sweet—sometimes.

Joanie said, 'I'll get the food ready. You go out and look around the garden, Penny. I want to heat up these Cornish pasties.'

Leo said, 'Let's pour the wine first. Where's the corkscrew?'

He poured four glasses of the cool white wine. Penny had already gone down to the edge of the lawn, where the little private jetty stuck out—a little rickety, but firm enough to hold the bobbing dinghy. Her name was *Marianne*. Penny gazed out at the blue lake, its surface broken by a thousand rippling waves, in the busy little breeze. Beyond, on the opposite shore, were autumn beeches in perfect gold, and then the bracken, and the sloping moorland.

Leo was standing there, handing her a glass of wine. 'Here's to beauty.'

'I'll drink to that,' Penny smiled. 'And to the *Marianne*. God bless her and all who sail in her.'

'The last person to say that was my mother,' he told her. 'It was her name.'

'Oh, I'm sorry.'

'I'm not. It was nice to hear you say the words.' He lifted his glass. 'To *Marianne*—and to Penny.' Then, in answer to her unspoken question, he went on, 'It was all a very long time ago. She was a lovely lady—

right to the end. Little Mrs Williams reminded me of her.'

'Is that why you sent me?' Penny breathed. 'Oh, Leo, why didn't you tell me?' She looked up at him. The breeze was ruffling his hair, giving him his natural outdoor look that she liked. 'You're such a nice man, Leo. Why aren't you married?'

He burst out laughing. 'That's what all Janet's bridge ladies are always saying, my dear! Only I don't tell them.'

'Are you going to tell me?'

'If you really want to know.'

'Yes.' She wondered if it would hurt her—if he would say that he was in love with Janet, but couldn't leave his father . . .

'I never met anyone I could love enough,' he said simply.

Penny breathed again. 'Is such deep love necessary? People marry for companionship, don't they?'

'Would you?' Leo asked.

'Oh no. But then I never thought of getting married anyway.'

'Never?'

'No. I'm content on my own,' she assured him.

'So am I.'

'But—' Penny thought again of the willing widow next door to Leo, 'you might be happier with someone to look after you.'

'No.' His voice was suddenly low and intense. The rippling waters lapped at their feet, and the soft chirruping of chaffinches in the trees was sweet all around them. 'That isn't for me. Marrying someone just to look after me is a violation of what marriage is about.'

She felt a little breathless at his vehemence, his passion. For a moment she saw clearly that he and Janet Rhys-Evans were from different planets. And why, suddenly, should the twinkling blue eyes of Robin White enter her head as they were talking of marriage? And Leo—a passionate marriage or none at all. It gave her a new facet of her chief to ponder over. She didn't realise she was silent, until Leo had asked her twice what she was thinking about.

'It's such a paradise here,' she told him. 'To think it's only two hours away!'

'Is that a signal that private thoughts are private?'

She faced him then. He was standing very close, and their eyes met in a long and significant look. 'Were you analysing me?' His voice was low.

'I don't think I could. You're very enigmatic.' She tried to make a joke, but her voice trembled a little at his nearness.

'Lunch is ready.' Gemma came running down to the lake to call them. 'Come and eat quickly—I'm dying to have a sail! It seems ages since summer, Uncle Leo, when we went out every day.' Penny was perhaps not surprised that Leo had taken Joanie and Gemma on holiday; it was so clear that they had a special relationship. A stranger would have taken them for a family.

'I hope you're a sailor, Penny,' said Leo, as they strolled up to the flat. Joanie had opened the french windows, and the meal was laid on the table, but chairs set out on the patio.

'I was born in Brighton, remember,' she reminded him. 'Not many people leave there without getting webbed feet.' She was looking forward to sailing more than she realised—the feeling of freedom, of freshness . . . 'I say, who would have thought we could eat out in October?'

'It'll be cold on the lake. I've got spare anoraks in the boat shed.' Leo was helping himself to sandwiches and a pasty. He sighed as he sat on the rustic bench outside. 'You see, Penny, how ravishingly beautiful the North of England is?' And she couldn't help but agree with him.

It was a bit of a turmoil in the boat, but Leo proved a good captain, and gave orders in a brisk determined way, so that they were obeyed instantly. The wind was cool and more playful than they expected, and for a while they were too busy getting used to the feel of sailing to have time to chat, but as they settled down to a good run before the wind, Penny had time to look around her. 'Oh, look!' she exclaimed suddenly. In the great expanse of blue above her, round the billowing sails, loomed the heather mauve moors. And above them was the magnificent shape of an eagle, wheeling majestically round the crags at the summit.

'I know it's a cruel bird,' breathed Gemma, 'but isn't it perfect? As though it were made for this place?'

'You wouldn't want him for a pet, eh?' smiled Leo, and crinkled his eyes again to gaze at the lovely creature.

'That would be very cruel. He belongs up there,' said Gemma firmly.

'Free. But I wonder if he's lonely?' Penny wondered.

Leo turned his attention back to his steering, as the boat lurched suddenly in a gust. 'His mate won't be far away. They won't be lonely.' And he looked at her as he said it, in a strange way, as though he meant more than he said.

Penny let her hand trail in the icy water, as a way of avoiding the disturbing look. 'I wish I could take home with me the perfect sounds of today. Just listen! Only the water, the sound of the sails, and the cry of the eagle. It's so deeply peaceful.'

'Recharges the batteries,' agreed Joanie, with her own more prosaic version of the scene. Her pale face was pink now with the wind and the excitement.

'Will there be time to climb a hill?' asked Gemma.

'It gets dark early. But perhaps a little one, if you aren't too tired when we start off home,' Leo told her.

'I'm a bit hungry again.'

He laughed. 'I know—you want to stop at that chip

shop on the way back! Don't worry, Gemma, it's on the agenda, if we go that way home.'

'Great!' Gemma settled back in the bows, looking out across the wavelets towards the opposite shore.

They had time to take a short walk after Leo had moored *Marianne* safely. Penny helped him with the gear, finding her heart full of delight at the unaccustomed activity and hard physical work. They climbed up the nearest mountain path. 'Just up to that plateau, no farther,' Leo warned. 'I have no torch, and I don't want to lose any of you.'

'I bet I get there first!'

'No contest,' laughed Joanie. 'I'll settle for halfway.'

'Penny?' Leo looked concerned.

'I won't settle for anything less than Gemma.' She put on a spurt, and almost caught her. 'You win,' she panted. 'I'm older than I look!'

Leo wouldn't let them rest. 'As soon as the sun goes down, I think we'll get some mist, as well as frost, so take care going down. You might twist an ankle in the dusk, and I can do without having to carry someone down.' But no one did, and he handed each of them down from the path over the final rock on to the road where he had parked the car. 'Chip shop next.'

'Yes, please!'

Gemma got into the back with her mother, who had the remains of the picnic in a basket, while Penny took the front seat. 'You certainly know how to please a lady,' she joked to Leo.

He started the engine, and smoothed back his tangled hair before sliding the Rover into gear. 'Fourteen-year-olds are easy—food and praise, lots of it. But I'm not sure about any older . . .'

'I don't believe you. You know everything. I've never seen you at a loss, Leo.'

'Well, I have—often.' He made the admission without selfconsciousness.

'You don't give that impression.'

'I suppose that's half the battle,' he agreed.

After supper of scampi and chips, Gemma fell fast asleep on the journey home. Joanie said, 'You must be very tired, Leo.'

'Yes. Isn't total exhaustion a wonderful feeling? You know you'll sleep well, and wake up refreshed. I love getting tired on my weekends off.'

Penny said, 'That's what I told you, isn't it?'

He grinned. 'Yes, Doctor. You certainly know your job!'

Joanie said from the back seat, 'I say, Penny, are you going to invite your Vicar friend to the surgery Christmas party?'

'What's that? Planning that already?' Leo's voice sharpened. 'What Vicar is that?'

'No one,' said Penny hastily. 'She's making fun of me. Do I have to come to the surgery party?'

'I haven't even started planning it yet. We usually have a social evening at one of the doctors' houses.' But he didn't pursue the subject, and nothing else was said as they sped through the night along the motorway back to Liverpool and reality.

Next day, Penny didn't wake up for a long time. When she finally opened her eyes, it was to a feeling of delightful languor. What a perfect day they had enjoyed! Her limbs ached a little, but it was a good feeling. And she had got on so very well with Leo Zander; they were almost friends. She had enjoyed the frank way he had chatted to her. She perhaps had got to know him a fraction more. Yet his secrets remained; he had cleared up none of them. The new facet he had revealed was his passion. She had never seen his eyes so animated as when he swore that marriage was worthless without turbulent attraction, passionate involvement . . . She wondered if Dai or Chris had any knowledge of that side of their chief, and decided not; it was the sort of thing only a woman could discern.

Yet the following weekend upturned this idea almost completely. Lil Donaldson had invited Penny for drinks. 'You were so kind over my little women's problem,' she told her. 'I shall be going to the gynae clinic next week. I didn't dare to tell the other doctors, but it's different with a woman.'

'I'm glad you came when you did.' Lil's trouble seemed minor, yet Penny was slightly worried that it had been going on so long without help. She certainly had a prolapse—but it was the slight bleeding occasionally that was the sinister element. It was good that the appointment was so quick; she had asked Mr David to fit her in as soon as possible.

'So you'll come?' urged Lil. 'Only close friends, as Sam isn't up to merrymaking?'

'I'm very honoured,' Penny smiled.

She arrived on time, as she knew that Sam, cheerful as he was, liked to go to his bed at a reasonable hour. As Lil greeted her, and introduced her to the neighbours, Penny realised that she knew quite a few of the people here, through Leo. She sat down, suddenly feeling that she was a stranger no more. 'That window-cleaner you recommended has been today,' Sam confided as he poured her a Martini. 'What a nice fellow!'

'Tim Watson? He's a joker, isn't he? I'm glad you liked him.' Tim was back at work after his fall from the ladder in James Street. His wife had complained to Penny that he ought to have claimed compensation for the fall, but Tim was too upright. It was his own fault, he said, and he refused to claim.

'Salt of the earth,' said Sam. 'Our last window-cleaner is in prison for theft. It's good to know there are still honest folk around.'

Someone else rang the bell, and Lil went to answer it. Penny heard the cultured contralto she knew so well;

Janet had a carrying voice. 'So terribly sweet of you to invite us!'

Penny watched the door from the corner of her eye. Yes, Janet Rhys-Evans swept in, magnificent in black pleated chiffon, her hair elegantly done, and her diamond earrings sending daggers of blue flame across the room. Leo Zander was close behind her, in dark suit and university tie, his hair sleeked back into his 'pillar of society' look. It was a different man from the one Penny had shared that sailing day with, and she looked at him as at a stranger. Janet held his arm. They were a couple, and she was having no one make any mistake on that, as she spoke of 'we' being delighted to see everyone. It was suddenly easy to believe. Penny's heart fell. Not that she minded, but she felt that Janet would not make Leo happy; he had almost admitted it. But he wouldn't let her hang on to him like that unless he wanted it too, surely?

'Leo, my old friend!' Sam reached out to shake his hand, but Janet took it first, and stood close by as Leo did the same, and patted Sam on the shoulder. 'Leo, I've just been talking to this lovely girl here.' Leo smiled at Penny and shook her hand too. Janet reached out and kissed her on the cheek, in a false gesture of affection. 'Leo, this girl is a jewel. I hope you're going to give her a permanent job. We can't afford to lose her, you know.'

Leo smiled. There was a murmur of approval from the people sitting close by, and they waited for Leo's answer. Penny's face flamed, and she looked at Leo, feeling sorry for him that he couldn't answer. She felt a sudden rush of—affection and warmth for him. Yes, it was affection. She understood how he felt at that moment, and her heart went out to him. She wanted to say, 'Tell them yes, Leo. I could work with you all my life.' But she knew it wasn't true. She would come to hate it, and it would be wrong to accept. To be kissed by Janet and her circle of friends, to be patronised by her.

Penny hid her eyes, so that Leo wouldn't see the warmth in them.

Leo handled it, of course; he always did. 'Decisions can wait till the new year, eh, Penny?'

Several people murmured a protest. 'You must know now,' they told him.

'I know, of course. But Penny is an independent lady. Our arrangement is until February, and I wouldn't dream of rushing her into an answer.'

Sam said in his rough but jolly voice, 'Come on, Penny lass, you're not going to leave us in the lurch?'

It was Janet's cut-glass bridge party voice. 'Women are not to be bullied these days, Sam. They're ambitious. If you were a brilliant doctor like Penny, with all sorts of medals and exams, would you settle for life at the docks? I know I wouldn't.' She smiled at Penny. 'You must decide for yourself, my dear. Your career must be your first consideration.'

Penny wished she would shut up. Her future was her own affair, and she was acutely embarrassed by the conversation. Leo was aware of her discomfiture, and changed the subject neatly by asking when the old school reunion was. Sam and his other old friends always managed to have a grammar school reunion. The laughter and banter turned to the ages of the 'schoolboys', and of their past exploits on the soccer and cricket fields.

Later, Penny found that Leo had escaped for a second. He was at her side, and he whispered, 'I'm terribly sorry about the personal talk. Sam's goodhearted, but he always speaks his mind.'

She looked up at him. She was suddenly choked by his kindness in taking the trouble to apologise; he was such a rock in times of trouble or discomfort—a rock in the unsettled stream of her life, that she thought she would quite like to cling on to for a while. If he had asked her at that moment, she would have agreed to stay on. 'It doesn't matter. I know them too, Leo, and I love them for their honesty.' She swallowed the lump in her throat. 'Thanks for being so tactful.'

'Penny, are you all right?' He put a hand on her arm. 'Can I——'

'Leo darling, I'm terribly sorry to rush you, but I think we ought to be going.' There was no need to look up to see who that was.

Leo took away his hand and put it over Janet's, which was hooked firmly in the crook of his elbow. 'Yes, of course, Janet. You're right, Mrs Banks will want to get home.' His tone and his look were warm to Janet. This woman did mean something to him; he allowed her to treat him as her property with no protest. And the way he spoke of letting Mrs Banks get home reminded Penny of a married couple speaking of the baby-sitter. Mrs Banks was certainly looking after old Dr Lionel. Perhaps this couple really were as close as Janet had implied. Perhaps she did not always go home . . . Penny moved away, making it very clear that she had no intention of monopolising Leo, and that he was free to go with Janet.

They went to the door together, and Lil gave them both a kiss. Yes, they were treated as a stable couple all right. Penny watched them go. This was the reality, not that sun-splashed day on the lake. Leo turned at the door, catching her staring. His dark eyes looked across the room, and for a moment everything else disappeared. She blushed, as though he had caught her in the act of admitting that she loved him. What nonsense! It was a word that could not be applied to him; he was too distant, too independent—like the wheeling eagle in the Cumbrian sky. Too far away . . .

Next day Chris Santani called on Penny again. She was slightly apprehensive, as the tall, slim figure was ushered in by Joanie. 'Hello, Chris,' she said. 'What can I do for you?'

'You wanted to borrow this paediatrics book,' he

explained. 'I've finished it, and it's very good.'

'Great—thanks,' she smiled. That was innocent enough. She had asked to borrow the book; it was the latest up-to-date authority, and she wanted to make detailed notes. 'Would you like a sherry?'

'Yes, thank you.' But as she went across the room to pour it, he followed her, and when she turned round, she found herself in his arms.

'Chris, no!' But her breath was taken away as his arms tightened. She was too amazed to struggle as his lips came down hard on hers, warm and abandoned. He pressed the length of his body against her, forced her lips open.

CHAPTER SEVEN

It had been a long week, and it had rained most of the time. Penny was used to it now. She accepted it, along with Chris's embarrassing attentions, and Dai's wild Celtic disregard for money. It was part of the Merseyside episode of her life, that had only a few more dreary weeks to run. Leo—Leo was the best part. He had taught her a lot, helped her a lot. She would miss Leo Zander when she left, but nothing else. Nothing.

Dai was his usual breezy self. She liked chatting to him after a busy surgery, because he could always find something to smile about. Penny was teasing him about trying to get out of doing a couple of calls. 'They're nice old dears, and it isn't urgent. They won't mind if I see them tomorrow instead,' he insisted.

'A date for lunch, is it, Dai?'

'Penny, my lovely, at my age all the best women have been snapped up. There's a shortage.'

'Not for a dashing young man with an Aston Martin?' she teased.

'Even that. What's the use of a passion wagon if there's no talent about to practise on?'

'Dai Richards, why don't you get yourself another hobby? It must be awful to have only one interest in life.'

'It is. Want to come for a drive, Penny? Ever been in an Aston?'

'No.'

'Don't you want to?'

'Not particularly. You know, you treat women as sex objects, Dai,' she told him. 'They don't enjoy that any more.'

He roared with laughter. 'Darling girl, are you telling

me? I have a bit more experience than you, and I haven't noticed.'

'All right, Mr Clever. Have you paid the practice back yet?'

Disconcerted, he said, 'Well, no. But at the end of the month . . .'

'You said that last month,' Penny reminded him.

'Well—' At her look, he said, 'Penny, at the moment I'm negotiating for a penthouse flat in the city centre —Albert Dock, actually—and I need a bit of ready cash for when I make the deal.'

'Dai, how could you?' But she wasn't really cross with him; it was friendly banter. 'Never mind, Dai, I'll treat you to lunch one of these days.'

'Promises, promises! You realise you're driving me into the arms of Andrea Mulhoney?'

'Reluctantly, of course.'

'Reluctantly. I protest every step of the way.'

Judy knocked on the door. 'Signed all your letters, Dr Harcourt?'

'Yes, thanks, Judy,' Penny said. 'You're looking a bit tense today. Everything all right?'

She was an ash-blonde, coming up to middle age. Judy was the quiet one, who let Kay do most of the shouting, but she could be firm too. Her face this morning was set and grim. 'Kay's not feeling well. I've been worked to death this morning while her ladyship drinks tea and takes Paracetamol.'

'Too bad.' Penny tried to be sympathetic. 'Never mind, we've all finished now. Let's look forward to Christmas. Where's the party this year?'

Judy's face cleared. 'We had it at a hotel last year. But Kay thinks we should have it at Dr Zander's this year, and get caterers in.'

'And what does Dr Zander think?'

'She hasn't told him yet.'

'Surely it's for him to decide,' observed Penny.

'Kay likes her own way,' said Judy petulantly. 'She's been with him the longest, and doesn't let him forget it.'

Penny tried to ease things. 'Judy, I find you all a close little circle. I suppose there are tensions, disagreements?' She was trying to reassure herself that she hadn't caused any of them.

Judy nodded as she gathered up Penny's letters. 'Yes, sure. Just like any family, I suppose. We have arguments —sometimes bad ones, but they sort themselves out.'

'I wonder how I fit in?' Penny asked.

Judy was flatteringly swift to answer. 'Just great! The patients love you—you should hear them!' She added quietly, 'And we hope you decide to stay too.'

'That's nice of you.' Penny smiled wanly. Chris's unwelcome attentions had nevertheless awakened strange signals in her body. It disturbed her, yet excited her as well. And the thought of meeting Robin White again was becoming gradually important to her as the days went by . . . All the same, it was nice to be wanted.

'Do you need me any longer?' Judy asked her.

'No, Judy, sorry. You go off—you look worn out.'

'Well, I've been doing two women's work.' Judy left the room with a pointed reference to Kay, and Dai grinned.

'They ought to put up for Oscars, those two!'

Penny smiled. 'It's a devil of a job, you know. They have to be the punchball in between us and the patients, and they can't please all the people all the time.'

'As they never tire of telling us.' Dai picked up his jacket and his call list. 'And less of this fishing for compliments, cariad. You know very well that everyone wants you to stay. I know damn well that you won't. We're a bit too plebeian for you, my lady—nothing personal, but I can just see your pretty nose turn up every time you see the muck in the back alley. Why not admit it?'

Penny felt as though she had been physically attacked.

'Is that what you really think of me?' she asked, hurt. 'That I'm stuck up? Do you think I don't care for my patients in the way that you three do?'

Dai paused on his way to the door, arrested by her sudden intense question. 'Well, yes, Penny—I wouldn't say it if I didn't think it. You're a damn good doctor, but James Street isn't for you.' He grinned suddenly. 'Of course, I have been known to be wrong about people! But—' he shook his head, 'sorry to say it, but I'm not wrong this time. See you, man.' And with a casual wave of the hand he left the room, the door swinging in his wake.

Penny stood for a moment. But there were too many calls for personal feelings to matter. She felt that Dai was wrong. She felt as though the patients were just as important to her as they were to Leo Zander. He had taught her that—by sending her to people like the Williams, and the Donaldsons—real people, whom she could not help but love. Penny banged the door with a certain annoyance as she left the surgery and checked her call list, to see which direction to take first.

She opened the car door, then she heard her name, and looked back. Leo stood at the surgery door. 'Penny, there's been a call from Debbie Grant—the baby. Do you want to see him, or shall I?'

'I'll go, of course. Is it his chest again? That's his weakness, little Jamie.'

Leo nodded. 'I thought you'd want to. Thanks, Penny.' It was only as she drove towards Dourton that she realised that she had proved Dai Richards wrong. Here she was taking on an extra call—and in the worst area—because of her personal commitment to Debbie and her little son. She smiled. That would be a point to score off Dai next time they met.

Dourton had not improved in beauty since she had been visiting it. But somehow the graffiti, the smells and the debris didn't matter to her, as she ran up the stairs to

the Grants' peeling front door. There were broken
windows on the staircase, and the wind whistled through
them. It was getting stronger. There would be a storm
soon. As always, scraps of dirty paper whirled in the air
like some dismal dervishes round the waste land with its
broken notice 'No Ball Games'.

Jamie was ill. He had a bad cough, which Penny
thought sounded frighteningly like the start of whooping
cough. 'Debbie, I think he'd be better off in hospital,'
she told her gently.

Tears came into the girl's eyes. 'Oh no, Doctor! I've
looked after him ever so well. Don't take him away!'
She clutched him to her, and Penny noticed that his
little white suit was spotless, that his dark hair was
clean and shining. 'I've been readin' up about proper
feeding.'

Penny understood. Debbie thought she had failed her
son. 'Deb, it isn't your fault,' she assured her. 'It's an
infection—most children come across it, but in Jamie's
case, because he does tend to get this sort of thing badly,
I'd like him to be in a place where he can be supervised.
But you must stay with him. They won't chase you away
at the hospital. They'll be delighted if you'd stay and
look after him.'

Debbie seemed to take it better. 'Then go ahead
and phone for admission. Me dad'll have to look after
himself a bit.'

'Is your mother not here?' asked Penny.

'Nah. I don't know where she gets to.' But Debbie
didn't seem to mind. Still holding Jamie close to her
breast, she smiled at Penny. 'This book's dead good
—tells you recipes for adults as well. I'm giving me dad
some, and he likes 'em. Cookin's int'resting.'

After arranging for Jamie's admission, Penny allowed
herself the luxury of staying and chatting to Debbie. It
was startling, the difference over a few short months.
Debbie had realised her own worth—possibly her

mother's absence had helped in that way—and was enjoying the new rôle of mother and provider. Penny had stopped comparing Debbie with the young mums of her last practice. She was just totally delighted by the improvement in her patient, and quick to give praise, that pleased Debbie so that her sallow cheeks tinged with embarrassment. 'It's you, really, Doctor, comin' so quick. I don't know what I'd'ave done without you to tell me what to do.'

In the blustering storm, Penny completed her calls. Joanie's flat was quiet without Gemma. After lunch she relaxed with *The Times*. It was even too blowy to take Bathsheba out. The rain was stinging on her cheeks, and she turned up the fire, glad not to be on call.

The rain and wind persisted. Leaves that had just turned autumnal in the parks were rudely torn from branches, turning the city from summer to winter in one week. The waves lashed the sea wall, sending spray yards over the promenade. Skies were angry, sunsets infrequent and luridly grim. Then a miracle happened that took Penny's mind off the weather. Robin White telephoned her at home. In an instant the surroundings vanished, and she felt a heartwarming glow suffusing her cheeks as she exclaimed, 'Robin, how nice to hear from you!'

'I haven't seen you around St Edmund's for a while.' He must have missed her, then.

'Well, Gordon is still in hospital,' she told him. 'His operation was a success.'

'That's good news. I did knock once or twice, but I suppose the brothers were hospital visiting.' Robin paused. 'Actually, Penny, I'm ringing to inflict a little more work on you—Tim Watson.'

'Tim? What about him? He's back at work, isn't he?' So it wasn't a social call, it was business. Oh well, it was still nice to hear his voice, to keep in touch.

'He is working, yes, and as cheerful as ever—I don't

know where he gets his good humour from. He's so
terribly pale, Penny, I'm sure he can't be well. I suggested he came to see you, but he said he was okay. But I
felt I ought to mention it.'

'I'll make a note to see him. Thanks, Robin. I did
wonder how he managed to fall from his ladder.
Apparently he used to be a river pilot—and they're
sure-footed if anyone is. There might be an underlying
cause. Well spotted, Vicar!' Penny wrote Tim's name on
her pad. 'And how is life with you?'

'Hectic. The ladies are preparing the hall for the
Christmas Fair—it's on Saturday. I don't suppose you'd
care to pop in?'

'I might if I'm in the area,' she told him.

'That's sporting of you. A church sale in the back
streets of Merseyside probably isn't your idea of a
swinging time, but we'd be grateful.'

Penny smiled as she rang off. It certainly wasn't her
idea of a perfect Saturday afternoon. But she remembered Robin's commitment—how he felt the call to stay
in Merseyside, to do what he could in his own small way.
If Robin White could do it, then Penny Harcourt could.
Dai's words about her stuck-up nose still rankled. This
was another way of showing him. She would go to the
church fair, and she would not only go, she would enjoy
herself. Smiling, she called through to Joanie, who was
writing letters in the other room.

'Joanie, how about taking in a church fair on
Saturday?'

'Are you serious?' Joanie called back.

'Of course. Don't you find Saturdays boring without
Gemma?'

'Yes. I was planning on having lunch in town.'

'Then let's do both—lunch in town, and St Edmund's
in the afternoon?'

With the Liverpudlian dry wit, Joanie said, 'You'd
better watch it, woman. High living on that scale'll do

you a mischief when you're not used to it. You'll need a double dose of Sanatogen.'

'I won't—but I've just been reminded of someone who does.' Penny picked up the paper with Tim Watson's name and address. 'I'd better go along and visit, there might be something serious here.'

'It's no fun going out on an afternoon like this.'

'Needs must, Joanie.' Penny pulled on her raincoat and pulled the collar up about her ears as she descended the stone steps to the car in the backyard of the dental lab. The technician was just going out too, a carrier bag in his hand.

'Hello, Doctor,' he greeted her. 'Just delivering a bagful of choppers.'

Penny giggled. Typically, the man made a joke out of a mundane life. 'Just like Santa Claus, doling out the happy smiles!' And he took a denture from the bag and said, 'Smile for the lady.' He got in the van, breaking into song as he passed her—'When Irish teeth are smiling . . .'

'Business must be good, Patrick,' Penny remarked.

'Mustn't grumble. All I want for Christmas is me two front teeth . . .'

The rain lashed at the windscreen as Penny made for the dockside area where Tim Watson lived. 'Just thought I'd pop in to see how the back is, Tim,' she told him.

'Couldn't be better, Doctor. I'm doing the north face of the Eiger next week. Nice of you to look in.'

'You are managing work all right? I know you can't go out in this, but if the weather is fair, you work an average day, do you?'

'Well, I've been slowing down a bit,' admitted Tim. His usually buoyant manner was a little subdued, his face pale, as Robin had noticed. 'Like a cuppa? Linda's at Bingo.'

'And what are you doing?' asked Penny.

'Well, I were just sitting, like. Lazy beggar, aren't I? It's all them wild women I call on, on me rounds.' Penny couldn't help smiling, in spite of her concern at his pallor.

'I want to take your blood pressure, and listen to your chest,' she told him.

'There's nothing wrong with me, honest.'

'Then unbutton your shirt.'

'You won't find anything.' But he did as ordered, taking off his shirt, and banging his chest like Tarzan, before an outbreak of coughing stopped him.

Penny found nothing abnormal, apart from a bit of bronchitis. 'Well, maybe after the chest is cleared, I'll permit the north face of the Eiger, Tim. But before that, will you go along to the hospital for a full blood count?' She scribbled the necessary forms. 'And a chest X-ray. This tiredness is probably nothing, but it does no harm to check.'

'What do you think I've got?' he asked.

'You might be anaemic, that's all.' But simple anaemia didn't occur in healthy males.

'That's all right, then,' Tim shrugged.

She saw that he had been hiding some worry, that she had allayed some of his fear. 'Is there anything you haven't told me?'

'Me clothes are a bit big,' he admitted.

'You mean you've lost weight? How much? How quickly?'

'A few months. Me appetite isn't what it was.'

Robin had certainly been right to draw her attention to this case. 'Well, you can stop worrying now,' Penny told him. 'Get the tests done, and we'll sort you out, Tim.'

'Okay. You're a good lass. You and Dr Zander've been good to me.'

'All part of the service,' she smiled.

But when she got back, she telephoned Leo's number.

There was nothing in Tim's notes, but perhaps Leo had noticed some clinical details. 'Hello? Leo?'

'Is that Penny? I'm sorry, my dear, but Leo is engaged. Can I give him a message?'

'No, thanks, Janet. I'll see him at surgery.' She was annoyed to find Janet there, queening it over Leo's home. Yet why should she mind? The woman was only being helpful. But what did 'engaged' mean? She must remember to ask.

It was still raining on Saturday, but the wind had dropped. The grey streets glistened damply, and the grey sky loomed over the drab city, dragging spirits down as the drizzle came inexorably down.

'Do you really want to go out?' Joanie's face was grey too, her hair straggly. 'Isn't it too much trouble, just to get wet?'

St Edmund's didn't mean quite so much to Joanie, Penny realised; she knew herself well enough to recognise the pull Robin White was exerting on her. It was Robin she wanted to see, not the church fair or Liverpool city centre on a wet Saturday. 'Please yourself. I think we'd feel better making an effort to enjoy ourselves.'

'Oh, all right. At least we ought to get a parking place in town—no one else in their right mind will be out.'

'How true!' Penny laughed. 'I'll take you to the Adelphi for a treat. You've cooked enough delicious meals for me, it's the least I can do.'

That made Joanie cheer up. She made up her face, and did her hair neatly. 'Now, is it cold enough for my fake fur?' Making the effort had already brought some colour to her cheeks.

As they sat back and ordered roast turkey and white wine, Joanie began to confess, 'It used to be fun, this time of year. It was the best time because Gemma used to be excited about Christmas. We used to see every Father Christmas in town, and visit all the grottoes.'

'And now you feel lonely and empty? Why don't you get a job? What did you work as before Gemma was born?' asked Penny.

'I'm a trained nurse—I was on the district for a while, then I left to nurse Leo's mother full-time. She was helpless at the end, but they didn't want her to go to a home, so I lived in.'

So Joanie had lived in Leo's house? Penny tried to stop the thoughts that came unbidden into her mind. Joanie must have been a pretty woman when she was younger. Even today, seeing her made up, taking care of herself, she didn't look her age. It wasn't hard to imagine a young doctor, a pretty nurse . . . Penny felt herself blushing, and applied herself vigorously to her chipolata sausage until the colour had subsided.

Joanie was scathing about the area of St Edmund's. 'What sort of bumper fun are we going to have here, then? Just look at that graffiti! It's pure filth, Penny.'

'But look at the pretty curtains in that terraced house —look at that new front door,' Penny pointed out. 'See how people keep up their self-respect, even in a place that looks bad at first.'

'You've changed,' said Joanie. 'You're actually sticking up for Merseysiders! Getting fond of town, are you—or just of the Vicar?'

Penny knew she didn't mean to be rude. 'Come on, Joanie, you're going to have fun, I promise. Look, there's the church hall.'

'Hm. The graffiti's even worse on that.'

Penny laughed. '"Warroirs kill". I wonder what warroirs are?' She led the way into the dreary wooden hut, where a damp banner proclaiming 'Christmas Fayre' hung limply over the door. 'Maybe those lads over there are the Warroirs—poor sad kids with no future and no aim.'

'Come on, Penny, let's get it over,' said Joanie firmly.

'Let's go and sample the home-made cakes.' They paid their twenty pence to a fresh-faced Girl Guide. There was no sign of young Robin White in the dark hall, but there was an immediate response from the first stallholder.

'Hello, Dr Harcourt! What are you doing here? It's really lovely to see you.' And within a few minutes Penny found she was besieged by patients, all touched and delighted that she had taken the trouble to come. 'Come and have some coffee. Our Tracy's on the cakes, she'll pick you some nice ones. You remember Tracy? You sent her for the tests when she had that rash. She's fine now. It was an allergy.'

Tracy brought them instant coffee, spilt in the saucers, and a plate of hardish scones. Joanie manfully ate one, with a wink at Penny. Penny was suddenly touched at the effort and the devotion that had gone into the decoration and stocking of these small, unimportant stalls. Worthy people all. She looked around, received more waves and compliments. She thanked Tracy, gave a generous tip, and said the scones were delicious.

The rain came down harder, drumming on the tin roof. Joanie whispered, 'I'm going to buy something. I'll see you in the car.'

'All right, I'll come. One round of the stalls and home.'

Joanie had already left the rickety little table, and Penny was just getting her handbag, when the sun came out in a blaze of glory—in other words Robin White appeared.

He was wearing his dog collar today, under a sweater. She thought it suited him. He sat down opposite to her, and immediately she forgot the rain and the dreariness of the day, as those blue eyes lit up the room for her. 'I honestly didn't think you'd trail here on such a rotten day,' he told her. 'I do appreciate it, Penny. It's really good to see you.' And he put his hand briefly over hers. Penny saw from the corner of her eye that Joanie was watching, and she looked away quickly.

'We haven't such a vast social life, Robin,' she explained. 'And I notice we share quite a lot of patients in common.'

He smiled. 'I won't argue with you about which of us does the most good.'

'Neither will I. But I'm glad you called me about Tim Watson.'

Robin looked gratified, and was leaning over to speak more, when his presence was requested by one of his ladies. 'Excuse me—I'm in demand, I'm afraid.' As he left, Penny felt a tug at her heart, and knew enough about herself to realise that this attraction could quite easily slip into love. She felt herself a fraud, being thanked by the ladies for coming, praised for taking the trouble. It was all because she liked Robin. Hormones had a lot to answer for! His animal attraction had added a fiver or so to the church funds, and Joanie was well aware of it. But she was goodnatured enough to make a joke out of it, as usual.

Holding up a highly coloured needlecase and a quilted tissue box cover, she said, 'I hope you realise what that man's fatal magnetism has made me buy!'

'It's very sweet of you to come,' Penny told her. 'It was fun, wasn't it? And it passed a rainy day. Your soul will have benefited.'

'My waistline hasn't—not after those scones!'

As they drove back, a pale watery sun made a shy appearance. 'Oh, look,' said Penny. 'It'll be lovely by the water. Shall we go down and watch the sun set?'

'No, Penny. Drop me at home, and I'll get dinner.' Joanie was not a sunset sort of person, as she freely admitted. So Penny left her at the flat, and drove down to the car park by the promenade.

The pale sunset was luminously lovely, a subtle yellow

light piercing the grey clouds and penetrating to the watery horizon, making a glimmering pathway across the estuary, and across the damp sands where the receding tide had left them. It was a gentle evening, after the misery and the drabness of the rain, a gentle and beautiful evening. Penny switched off her engine and locked the car, strolling along by the railings, breathing the calm air deeply, relishing the almost total silence, but for the call of the gulls along the edge of the water.

Suddenly she recognised the tall figure in a blue anorak coming towards her, his dark hair gently disturbed by the soft breeze. She saw him recognise her and the smile spread from the dark eyes to his lips. 'Hello, Penny!' Leo greeted her.

'Hello. I didn't expect to see you here.'

'I do live here,' he smiled. 'You look lonely, Penny.' They were facing each other, both still rather surprised to have run into each other. He turned and looked out over the estuary, leaning his elbows on the railing, and Penny joined him there, feeling suddenly glad to have met a friend. 'Have you had a lonely day?'

'No, I've loved my day,' she said, with more enthusiasm than she meant to express. Then she realised she would have to explain further, and how did she do that without revealing that it was Robin White who had made her day lovely? By changing the subject, of course. 'You look lonely too,' she remarked.

He smiled. 'I'm just one of life's loners, Penny. I often come down when I feel caged in the house.' She looked at him sideways, as he stared out towards the horizon, glorious in pinks and yellows. His profile was perfect. Her eye for beauty was quite captivated for a second, and she caught a glimpse of that passionate and untameable nature of his, reminding her of the eagle they had seen circling the Cumbrian mountain.

'Are you happy?' she asked suddenly.

He turned and smiled at the abruptness of her question. 'My father always told me that true happiness only comes out of doing what's right.'

'And that's what you're doing?'

'Perhaps,' he shrugged.

'And it's not working?'

'Hey, Penny, stop analysing me! I didn't say I wasn't happy.'

'No.' But he looked it, she thought. She suggested brightly, 'Perhaps it's right to look for happiness? It's your duty.'

'Put like that, my philosophical friend, then it is my duty.' Leo smiled again, and took her arm. 'Come on. We've seen the sunset, now come back and have a drink with me. That *will* make me happy!'

Penny found herself walking alongside him, climbing up over the grass, a short cut to his home, just across the road. She made no protest. She enjoyed talking to Leo when he was in this easygoing frame of mind. In fact, she had to admit that she enjoyed Leo Zander's company. It was something she would miss a lot. He had become a very important figure in her life—the one she always turned to. She would miss him—for a little while . . .

He opened the door with his latchkey and ushered her inside, holding out his hand for her coat. She was wearing a simple grey flannel skirt and a white sweater, and at first it felt quite smart—until Janet Rhys-Evans appeared in the hall. 'Oh, you're back, Leo dear. Dinner's nearly ready.'

Penny's heart sank. 'Hello, Janet,' she said.

'Hello, my dear. How nice to see you again.' Her cream wool dress and tan patent shoes looked like a study from *Vogue*. Penny looked down at her skirt, and felt like a country cousin.

Leo explained—as though he had to explain to Janet, 'Penny was wandering by the beach like Mary calling the cattle home, so I thought a stiff drink was required.'

Janet took over. 'Of course it was. Come in, Penny. Sherry, or something stronger?'

She was a charming hostess too. She was certainly very much at home among Leo's drinks. Penny had no choice but to sit down and make small talk with Janet. Leo interrupted, 'I'll get them. Try a small whisky and soda, Penny—takes the chill from the end of your nose.'

'All right.' Leo poured them each a drink. 'I'll just see if Father's all right—back in a tick.' He took a tumbler with a little whisky with him, and Penny watched him, recalling his moment of turmoil. One of life's loners . . . He was caged here. Comfortable, but caged . . .

He returned quickly. 'I'm not quite sure what's happening in the kitchen. Could you check, Janet?'

'Of course.' She seemed proud to be needed. 'Excuse me, Penny.'

Penny remembered the evening when Janet had been the visitor, when Leo had invited Penny for supper. She smiled rather wickedly. 'Don't worry, Leo, I won't stay and let your dinner spoil.'

To her surprise, he put a hand against her cheek, tipped her face up towards him. It was an intimate gesture, showing that they shared a secret as they shared a smile. 'You're very welcome to stay for dinner,' he told her.

'Thank you, but I have other plans.' Joanie was preparing a meal. But the way Penny said it caused an unspoken question to form in Leo's face: he was curious as to who was sharing Penny's evening. Penny smiled and didn't tell, teasing him a little.

'Have another drink, Penny.' Janet came bustling back, every inch the middle-class hostess.

'No, thank you. I'll be late.' She discerned a small look of relief in Janet's face.

Leo came with her to the door. 'I wish you were staying. You lit up my evening more than the sunset did,' he said, unexpectedly gallant.

'You know, you did too.' Penny found herself blushing, not knowing why she had to be so honest with him. But it brought a light to his eyes that she hadn't seen before. Then he bent and kissed her cheek once, twice —three times . . . 'Good night, Penny my dear.'

CHAPTER EIGHT

PENNY and her colleagues were far too busy the following week to have time to make comparisons. But if she had, she would scarcely have recognised her smooth-haired, dark-suited chief from the casual and amusing Leo she had enjoyed the evening with. His dark head was invariably bent—over letters, notes or patients. He issued his directives with curt sentences. He controlled the uproar in the waiting room when Kay declared she could no longer cope. And he quietly but firmly put Dai Richards in his place when he complained at having to take a call that was at the opposite side of town.

As if the week wasn't busy enough, on Wednesday the pipes burst. Penny arrived to find a stream of water pouring down the stairs, being directed out of the front door by Kay with a broom, while the patients stood outside in a bewildered group, the queue growing longer by the second. The morning was cold and damp, with a slight mist. Penny said, 'I'd better send the patients home. Let me speak to the ones who can't wait, and take the addresses of those we can visit later.'

'We can't visit fifty people,' protested Dai, appearing at the door with his trousers rolled up to his knees.

Leo said briskly, 'We aren't going to, Dai. Go ahead, Penny—you assess the urgent ones, and ask the others to come back tomorrow. I can't see us being able to clear this up by evening.'

At that moment the plumbers arrived in their van, and jumped out. The leader of the three men asked, 'Right, now, who does this place belong to?'

Leo said, 'It belongs to the firm next door. Does that matter now?'

'Can't do anything without permission of the owner.'

The water continued to trickle out. Leo said, his voice quiet but very firm, 'Get on with it. The manager will come over as soon as he gets here—meanwhile this is an emergency.' And something in his manner overruled the plumber's reluctance to disobey the regulations. The men disappeared up the stairs.

By the end of the morning, Penny had dealt out prescriptions on the pavement, and made a list of calls that she considered urgent. The others had gone to the aid of Judy and Kay, and spent the morning wringing out cloths and towels, as they surveyed the mess caused by the flood. 'Oh, for a nice modern health centre!' moaned Dai.

Leo said, 'Look on the bright side. This disaster means we'll have to have some urgent repair work done. We'll try to modernise a bit if the firm next door will let us.'

It was Chris Santani who pointed out that the entire building was Victorian. 'If you mend the pipes and cistern, you will find something else will go. The roof is leaking in the stock room, and my walls are very damp.'

Kay turned up, her hair damp and tangled. 'Doctor, we've done all we can. Can't you ring the cleaner to come? I'm creased!' She leaned the broom against the wall. 'This is all we need!'

Leo ushered them all into his room, when the carpet had been rolled up, the floor still damp, but useable. 'I wonder if there's any chance of coffee. We could do with it.'

Penny said, 'I don't think I have time. There are a few calls here I ought to see. Mrs Wilks is having breathing problems. Can I take a few of these calls, and leave you to sort out the others between you?'

Leo took the long list from her. 'You look worn out, Penny. It isn't often you see all your patients standing up. Yes, you go and see Mrs Wilks.' As she left, he said,

'Oh, and Tim Watson's results are here. I haven't had time to look at them. Take them with you.'

She was glad to get away from the scene of devastation. Even with a list of a dozen calls, at least she didn't have to look at that hopeless sight, at her colleagues sitting around like refugees. She went to Mrs Wilks first, and gave her an injection of Aminophyline. Then she sat for a while in the car, arranging the calls into some sort of logical order, so that she made no U-turns, and covered each district without having to go back again. Time passed. She forgot to look at her watch, as she systematically worked her way through the list.

She reached the last name on her list, crossed it off with a firm line of her pen. Thank goodness! She was very hungry. She looked at her watch! It was three o'clock in the afternoon. No wonder she was hungry —and thirsty—and tired . . .

At that moment she spotted the envelope on the floor with Tim Watson's blood test results. Oh well, better see him before going home. She slit open the letter. His blood picture was almost normal. Nothing at all—no anaemia, no abnormality of red cells, to account for his loss of weight and his tiredness. She straightened her aching back. Just one last call . . .

'Hello, Tim,' she smiled as he opened the door.

'Come on in, Dr Harcourt,' he invited.

'Well, your blood tests are okay, Tim.'

There was a snort from the back of the room, and Tim's plump little wife appeared. 'He wants to laze around the house all day, that's his problem, Doctor!'

'Well,' Penny smiled wearily, 'there are a few more tests we can do. I'd better take another look at your chest, Tim. How's the cough?'

'Seems to be easier, Doctor.'

She examined him again, then she filled in a form for a thyroid function test. 'I'd go along with this today, Tim,' she advised.

'Why the rush?' His face was apprehensive.

Penny managed to make a joke of it, hide her worry. 'With your wife in that mood, Tim, you're best to get out from under her feet!'

He laughed. 'Good thinking, Doctor. I'll get the next bus.'

And so Penny found herself sitting in her car, doing a fair imitation of a damp rag. It was too late to think of lunch. St Edmund's Vicarage was just up the road, and suddenly she felt a surge of energy. She would call on Robin, tell him the progress report on Tim Watson—it really was only right, after he had drawn her attention to the man. She drove quickly the last few yards up the street, got out, and walked up the Vicarage path with a light heart. Robin always made her feel better.

At the end of the leaf-strewn path, the Vicarage door loomed large and solid wood. Penny rang the bell.

The curly-haired woman who answered the door was Penny's age, and she had a small rosy child under one arm, resting contentedly on her hip. 'Hello,' she said. I'm Ann White. I'm afraid Robin's in a meeting.'

Penny felt as though someone had punched her very hard in the stomach. She took a step back, then regained her self-control. 'I'm Penny Harcourt—Dr Harcourt. Nice to meet you.'

'Oh, come on in. Is it about a patient?'

Penny swallowed. 'Yes. Tim Watson.' She felt herself gabbling. 'But it isn't important, Mrs White. I'll see him again.'

The young woman smiled. 'Do come in. The place is in a bit of a mess—it usually is with this scamp about!' She shook the little boy and gave him a cuddle. 'Have a cup of tea with me?'

'Oh, but——'

'No, please. It's nice to have company. Robin's always out visiting. And the kettle has just boiled.'

The thought of tea was too tempting to the weary

Penny, and she followed Anne White into the Vicarage.
'It's kind of you. I am tired,' she admitted. 'We've had a
traumatic day.' And over tea, Penny found herself
chatting quite naturally to Robin White's wife.

She had assumed too much. Robin had never acted
in any way—had he?—to make her think he was un-
married. Yet he had invited her for drinks, more than
once. Had he really thought it didn't matter? Surely a
young man of Robin's intelligence knew exactly what he
was doing? Penny felt her feelings doing somersaults.
She hadn't really done anything embarrassing—yet she
felt uncomfortable sitting in Robin's kitchen drinking
Robin's tea with Robin's pretty wife and cute little son.
'I must be going,' she said, getting up.

'Do come again. It was nice chatting.' Ann White was
open and friendly. They had a lot in common. Yet Penny
knew that she would pay less attention to St Edmund's
from now on. She drove off, feeling pink and clumsy,
like a teenager who didn't know where to put herself.

Robin White—a married man. Happily married. The
thought of the two of them together . . . There was a
sudden shrill scream, and Penny jammed on the brakes,
as a small figure ran out into the path of her car in the
increasing dusk. She swerved and brought the car to a
stop facing the opposite way. The child lay in the gutter,
terribly still. It was a boy, of about five or six, with fair
hair and grey dungarees. He lay like a crumpled doll, his
eyes closed.

Penny got out of the car, her eyes glazed, her feelings
numb, as a woman came running up. 'I saw it—it wasn't
your fault. Gary ran straight out without looking.'

Penny knelt by the little body. 'I'm a doctor.' She
gently felt his limbs, but nothing was broken; she had felt
no bump. His face was unmarked, but there was a small
graze on the side of his head. She felt slightly sick, but
she went on with her examination.

Another figure threw herself down beside the child,

crying, 'What will I tell his dad? Oh, Gary love, wake up!'

The other woman said, 'The car didn't hit him. He must have twisted his ankle getting away from it, and hit his head on the kerb.'

The mother sobbed, 'This is a play street. He never would have expected any traffic.'

Penny said, finding her voice sounded very far away, 'I know. I was only doing about fifteen. I think he's just concussed. I'll take you both to Casualty. He'll need a skull X-ray, but I think everything should be all right.'

The helpful woman said, 'You go, Phyll. I'll tell Harold where you are, and that there's nothing to worry about.'

'There might be, though.' But at that moment the boy stirred, coughed, then vomited. Penny turned him on his side, to keep his airways clear. 'There, he's bad!' exclaimed his mother.

'No, that's quite common with concussion. Would you hold him in the back of my car? I'll get you to hospital as soon as possible. They'll want to observe him overnight, but I think he'll be all right.'

The woman lifted Gary, and silently sat in the back as Penny drove as though part of a nightmare, along the now lit streets to the hospital. Her actions were cool and collected, but her mind was in a turmoil. The mother, Mrs Seaman, sat with a grim face; there was nothing to say. She might have lost her son. It might have been his fault, but a life lost can never be brought back. When they got to the hospital, Penny ran to get a porter with a trolley. 'RTA,' she said urgently. 'Concussion, I think.'

The mother walked alongside the trolley, holding Gary's hand, tears streaming down her cheeks. Gary, however, was feeling better, and smiled at the porter, telling him in a proud voice that he'd been knocked down by a silver-coloured Metro. The casualty officer was waiting in a cubicle. He said gently to Penny and Mrs Seaman, 'If you'd just wait in the waiting room.'

Penny left the mother for a moment. 'I must just make a phone call,' she said. She dialled Leo's home number. There would be no one at evening surgery, because of the burst pipes.

'Dr Zander?' his voice answered.

'Oh, Leo, it's Penny.'

'I know—I can tell your voice.'

'Leo—' to her horror, she heard herself dissolving into tears. 'I'm at the hospital. I knocked a child over—only concussion, but——'

'I'm on my way.'

Penny went back to sit by Mrs Seaman. It was still a nightmare—but knowing that Leo was coming made it bearable. Mrs Seaman had helped herself to a coffee from the machine. She pointedly didn't offer one to Penny, who sat with eyes unseeing, staring into space.

The casualty officer came towards them. 'He's quite all right, Mrs Seaman—no fractures. But we'll observe him overnight, just to make doubly sure.'

'Can I stay with him?' she asked.

'Of course. The porter will take him up to the ward shortly.' Mrs Seaman turned and left Penny without another word, and the casualty officer looked at Penny. 'You were the driver?'

'Yes—I'm Dr Harcourt. He ran out . . .'

'I'm Dr Charles.' The young man shook her hand. 'Not a pleasant experience.'

He wasn't blaming her. She felt tears well up in her eyes, and turned away. 'No.'

'Can I get you anything?' he offered. 'It must have been a shock?'

'No, thank you. I'll be off, then.'

He shook her hand again. 'Take care, Dr Harcourt.'

Penny turned and walked blindly in the direction of the entrance. She desperately wanted to cry, but that would be foolish in full view of the waiting room. She must get back. But her hands were suddenly trembling violently, she couldn't drive in this state.

Then two strong arms enfolded her in a sturdy and reliable embrace. 'It's all right, Penny—I've got you.'

'Oh, Leo, thank God!' she exclaimed.

'You look as though you're in a trance.' He led her gently towards his car. 'I'll send Banks to pick up your car later.'

'Wait—the drug bag—in the boot——' she protested.

'I'll do it. Give me the key.' Leo put her carefully in the front seat of the Rover, then went off to collect her drug bag and sphyg. 'There, now you can relax. I'll take you home where I can look after you.'

'I'll be okay,' Penny told him.

'Not in Joanie's little place you won't. I want to keep an eye on you.'

She kept quiet, knowing that she was glad to be taken care of, but also embarrassed and ashamed that the accident had been partly her own fault. She had been in some kind of dream state, still reeling with the shock of finding out that Robin was married. She must take the blame. Guilt overwhelmed her, and she covered her face with her hands and sobbed.

Leo picked her up and carried her into his house, putting her down on a chair, and allowing her tears to subside naturally. He went to the kitchen and quietly brought her a large mug of hot tea. 'When did you last eat?' he asked.

'I missed lunch—so many calls. I wanted to get them done.'

'That's why this happened—too tired.'

'No, Leo, not tired,' she sighed. 'There were other things——'

'Do you want to talk about it?'

'I don't want to be a nuisance.'

'Penny, you would never be that.' In the midst of her grief, she still recognised something terribly tender and vulnerable in Leo's voice. She looked across the room. He was sitting opposite her, his dark eyes filled with concern. She was conscious of the darkness outside, the distant crashing of the waves. The tide must be up.

'I could have killed him.' She spoke in a low voice, coming to terms with her situation. 'I could easily have killed him.'

'But you didn't. He's going to be all right.'

'Leo, you were right about pre-menstrual tension. It's that time of the month with me—that, plus personal problems——' Suddenly she burst out with, 'You should never have taken a woman partner! I've caused you only trouble.'

He came to her, sat on the arm of the chair, and held her close against him. Penny allowed herself to be held, to bury her face against his warm comforting pullover. 'No, dear, no trouble, you'll see. Once you've got over the shock, you'll see—no trouble at all.'

'Leo, I must tell you everything,' she faltered. 'It was—about a man—a man I cared about——'

She felt his body tense, but he didn't take his arm away. 'Yes?'

'I found out that he's married.' The words came out with a rush. 'Married to such a nice wife . . .'

Still tense, his voice distant, he said, 'I understand.'

Penny extricated herself from his embrace, looked up at him with tearful red eyes. 'Leo, don't be so nice to me. Shout at me—tell me I'm an idiot, and that I've let you down. Tell me what a stupid gullible fool I've been, and that I've no right to have such a good man as you for a friend.'

Leo took her face in his hands, his touch very light, his eyes very gentle. 'Why should I do that, Penny?' There was a slight smile in his eyes. 'You're doing such a good job yourself, there's no need for me to say anything.'

His easy manner helped her, and she felt herself calming down, reassured by his presence, by his closeness. 'Why are you so nice to me?' she asked tearfully.

'Because you've done nothing at all that annoys me. You've been through a bad patch. In the morning it will all be like a dream, and you'll feel better, I promise that, Penny. And we'll say no more about it, unless you want to.'

The back door banged and Leo said calmly, 'That will be Mrs Banks. I'll just let her know you're staying for supper.'

'There's no need——' Penny began.

'And the night. The spare room is made up.'

But it was Janet's bell-like tones that rang through the house. 'Anyone home?'

Leo shot up, and hurried to the door. 'Hello, Janet. I say, I hope you don't mind, but we've had a bad day, and I—well, I'm rather tied up.'

'I can't help at all, then, Leo? Father all right?'

'Yes, thank you, angel. See you tomorrow.'

Angel. Penny smiled a trifle grimly. All the same, Leo had got his own way. She heard Janet's high heels tapping away down the back path. Leo came back. 'Drink, Penny?'

'Please.'

He gave her a small whisky. 'I'll just see to Father. Back in a few minutes.' But before he had been gone a minute, Penny's head had fallen on her arms, and she was fast asleep, worn out with the emotion and trauma of the day.

'Are you awake?' Leo's voice brought her back to reality.

She sat up. 'Oh, I'd forgotten . . . I'm sorry . . .'

'It's okay.' He came across. 'You're looking better. You were so sound asleep, when I came back earlier on, that I left you to it.'

She took a deep breath. 'I am better, thank you. It must be late. I must go.'

'It's nine o'clock in the evening. Dinner is ready, and Mrs Banks has gone home.' Leo held out his hand. 'Come on now, Penny, a good meal and then a long sleep—doctor's orders.' She was going to protest, but he silenced her quickly. 'No more nonsense about being in my way—I'm delighted to have your company. It's time you knew that by now.'

She did feel more normal. It had been the accumulation of tiredness, caused by working too hard, plus the shock of the accident. 'I know, and I'm grateful. I'll try not to talk any more nonsense.' She managed to smile at him, and was glad to see a relaxed Leo smile in return. 'You know, I will miss you when I leave,' she confided.

'You will?'

She nodded, as they went through to the dining room, where a joint of roast pork lay on the hotplate, with dishes of vegetables, gravy and stuffing. 'I say, this is a feast! Are you sure no one else is coming?'

'Quite sure. Go on about missing me.' Leo filled her plate and poured sparkling wine into a crystal glass. 'Come on, you can talk with your mouth full.'

Penny did her best to obey. 'I'll miss everybody, I suppose. It's only natural, when you've got to know such a practice. And Dai—he's so goodhearted really. And Chris—well, I don't really know Chris very well—' she lowered her eyes. There was no need to tell Leo about Chris's advances to her. But Leo spotted her change of tone. He was so kind, so dependable. Penny knew she had got over the shock of the accident because he was with her.

'Well,' he said, and his voice was liquid honey, 'you're welcome to stay on with us—I hope you know that. But I'm not going to pressure you in any way. It has to be your own unaided decision. The rest of your life matters.'

'I suppose you'll want to look out for a replacement for me early in the new year?' she asked.

He was silent. Penny looked up from her plate and saw that he was looking at her with one of his unreadable looks. She told him so, and he shrugged his shoulders. 'There's no harm in admitting it—there is no replacement for Penny Harcourt. No one has her sweet nature, her soft voice. No one has her natural looks, her blue eyes and her untidy hair. No one has her strength of character, her guts, and no one has her compassion. There's no one who can take her place.'

'Leo.' Her voice croaked in her throat, and she tried again. 'Leo, don't talk like that! It isn't . . . well, you shouldn't . . .'

'Shouldn't what? Tell you how nice you are? Why not?'

'We were talking about doctors, not men and women.'

'Oh well, in that case I'll get another doctor when you leave, no problem.' Leo allowed himself to smile a fraction. 'Will that do?'

'Yes,' she whispered. But his words had upset her, awakened her. She put down her fork. 'I can't manage any more, I'm sorry,' she apologised.

'It's all right. Come through to the lounge and look at the river by night. I won't make coffee, because I want you to sleep soon, but I'll warm some milk.'

'No, please, I don't want anything else.'

'Come through, then.' He waited for her to rise from the table. She was very aware of the silence of the house, of the fact that they were alone together, and that she was as conscious of Leo's attraction as he had made it clear he was of hers. She tried to avoid his touch as they went through to the other room.

The curtains were open, so Leo did not put on the light, and they stood for a moment, watching the river, the sky with a few stars showing between ragged clouds, the flickering lights on the Cheshire side of the estuary.

He stood by her, and his arm went round her shoulders —loosely, with no pressure—just as good friends might stand, admiring a scene together.

Penny tried to remind herself of all the reasons why she ought not to be cementing any relationship with this man. He was a loner, he was practically engaged to the woman next door, he was paying the school bills for an illegitimate child, he was the boss she was going to leave soon, and ought not to become attached to in any way in case it swayed her professional judgment to leave.

He moved away suddenly, and she looked after him, unwilling to admit that she wanted him back, that she felt safe, contented, at peace with him. But he was back in a moment, holding a glass. 'Have a nightcap,' he offered.

'No, thank you.'

'It will help you to sleep. I'd like one.'

'All right,' Penny shrugged.

He poured a second glass for himself, added ice and soda, then he came back to stand beside her, looking down, making her feel small and vulnerable and in need of comfort. She sipped the whisky, and it warmed and burned her throat. Then she stopped feeling self-conscious. She sighed and said, 'Well, I've been two kinds of a fool today. I don't know how you've done it, Leo, but you've made me feel like a human being again. Thank you for that.'

'You're welcome,' she smiled.

'If I hadn't been here, would Janet have dined with you?' she asked.

He shook his head. 'No. She isn't a regular, you know. She just pops in—it got to be a habit after her husband died. I knew just how desperate loneliness can be, and I made it clear that I didn't mind if she wanted to talk, so she does.'

'And she helps with your father.'

'Sometimes. She's a good soul.' Yes, he had called her angel . . . He said, 'Why do you ask?'

'Just so that I know I'm not interrupting any of your plans.'

'Penny, don't say that!' He sounded quite hurt. 'You know you're welcome here any time.'

'Thanks.'

'You once said you didn't know me, Penny,' he went on. 'Do you know me now?'

She couldn't answer him. 'I know enough to like you very much. As a doctor—and as a friend——'

'Is that all?' Leo's voice was deep and almost purring as he took away the glass from her hand. Before she could think of a reply, he had kissed her, his arms gently enfolding her, at first like cobwebs, so delicate was their hold. Then, when she made no objection, when she returned his kiss, suddenly rapturous at its sweetness, their embrace became impassioned, unbelievably intense. Penny's head spun. This was a reality she had not known before, a part of her education she knew about only in theory. And it was with a great reluctance that she obeyed Leo, as he gently unwound her arms from his neck and said, 'You must go to sleep now.'

CHAPTER NINE

WHEN Penny awoke next morning, her first thought was that she must get back to her flat. What would people think if they saw her and Leo leaving the house together? Yet she felt languorous, and her heart was strangely peaceful. Something had happened in her life that had awakened her to a new wisdom, a new maturity. Robin White? Yesterday she had been fond of him; today he was just another name to her. Gary Seaman? He would be all right today. Nevertheless, she telephoned the hospital from the bedside phone, and had her optimism confirmed. Yes, he had had a peaceful night, and was going home with his mother as soon as they had eaten breakfast.

Leo Zander? So kind, so gentle—had he really said all those nice things about her? She put her hand to her mouth, touched her cheek where she had felt his warm breath, before he kissed her. She was filled with affection, and with an enormous gratitude. He must have said those things to help her over Robin. She looked at her watch—seven. Good, she had time to dress, to get away before the usual commuters started appearing in the road, on the way to the station.

She washed quickly in the little bathroom adjoining the spare room, making as little noise as possible. She took off the pyjama top Leo had lent her, and dressed in her own clothes.

She tiptoed to the front door. There was no sound from any other room as she opened the door. Her car was there, brought back by Mr Banks last night. Penny collected her drug bag and sphyg that Leo had left in the hall, and made her way back to Joanie's, as silently as she could. The roads were deserted, the sun sparkled on the water. Even the docks looked lovely in the morning haze, the great blue cranes standing like so many sleepy monsters, waiting to be woken. Her feeling of elation persisted. Dear sweet Leo, to have given her so much of his attention when she needed it—to have made her feel wanted, protected, safe.

'Hello, Joanie,' she called as she walked into the house.

'Morning, Penny. Night call?'

'You could say that. The toast smells wonderful!'

Leo was his usual self when they met the following morning after surgery. The decorators were in, repairing the mess made by the flood, but the doctors had managed to get through the patients without too much discomfort. Penny's room was at the front, away from the flood, but Dai's and Chris's rooms were messy, the walls streaked with damp, the paper falling off the walls.

He smiled at her across his room. 'Morning, Penny. You're looking well today.'

'I'm fine, thank you.' And she meant it. Leo nodded, reading her look, and the warmth in her voice.

'How are you, Dai, Chris?' he asked.

'In my usual rude Welsh health, thank you, Leo. Why the query?'

Leo smiled. 'I've been invited to Paris. I've a friend there, who isn't using her flat in the Champs Elysées. Do you think you could manage without me for a week?'

'We could, but I can't answer for the patients,' joked Dai. 'No, you go. You haven't had a break for ages.'

'We did agree not to take holidays in winter, because of the heavier surgeries.' Leo wasn't sure. 'I'll leave it a week or two. So long as I've warned you that I might just take off if things seem quiet.'

He pulled the call book towards him and ticked off the ones he would be doing. The telephone went, but Kay must have answered it in the office, for suddenly she burst in, her face white. 'Dr Zander, it's Mrs Rhys-Evans. Your father's collapsed! She's sent for the ambulance.'

Leo jumped to his feet. Penny reached over and took the list of calls from his hand. 'You go—we'll do these,' she said quickly.

'Thanks, Penny.' He grabbed his bag and was gone.

'Poor old fellow! But he's had a good innings.' Dai began copying his calls. 'Leo's been more than good to him.'

'It is a good thing this did not happen when he was in Paris,' said Chris Santani. He reached out and took Leo's list from Penny's hand. 'Come on, Penny, you can't do them all yourself. Let us share them out.'

'Thank you.' Penny waited until the calls were sorted out. She was wondering who this 'she' was who owned a flat in Paris, and was on such good terms with Leo . . . But why wonder? he was a very attractive bachelor, and no one like that lived like a monk. She must expect him to have admirers in many places.

Dai said, 'I wonder if it's any use phoning the hospital? The old man'll be in intensive care, I guess.'

Chris agreed. 'We'd better get the calls done, keep the wheels oiled for Leo, so that he doesn't have to worry about anything else.'

'You're right. But as he's eighty-nine, I can only think that the next item on the agenda will be funeral arrangements.'

'Don't say that!' Penny had become fond of the old man, silent though he was; he was so dignified, in spite of his blankness. And she had heard a lot of his past kindnesses from Joanie. True, he had educated Leo in duty, in the pursuit of what is right, not what is fun. But he had made his son into a wonderful man, and a great doctor. 'Poor Dr Lionel,' she said softly.

The phone rang, and Dai grabbed it. 'Yes?' There was a brief exchange, and the Welshman put down the phone. 'Heart attack—died instantaneously. You couldn't wish him a happier end, Penny.'

'No,' she agreed.

'Is there anything we can do?' asked Chris.

'No. He said just to get on with a normal day. Put a notice that he won't be taking evening surgery.' Dai pressed the bell to let Kay know.

They were just leaving the surgery when the second post arrived. Penny waited to see if there was anything important, and pounced on Tim Watson's chest X-ray. The others had gone as she read the radiologist's report. 'Shadowing in left base, probably tuberculosis. Suggest immediate referral to chest physician.'

'Oh, poor Tim!' She scribbled his name on her call list, but there was no need, as she went to see him first. She made an urgent appointment with the hospital before she left the surgery, and wrote a note for Tim to take with him. She didn't tell him the diagnosis. 'The X-ray showed shadowing in the lungs, Tim. Nothing scaring —it can be treated. Pop along to the clinic next Friday.'

The funeral of old Dr Lionel was on Friday. It was arranged for noon, so that all four partners could attend. They made their several ways to the big church near the river, where Dr Lionel used to be a sidesman. Penny was not surprised to find it full to the doors.

Dai saw her coming, and waited for her. 'One or two people here today,' he commented. 'I guess old Lionel brought half of them into the world.'

'He must have been a character,' said Penny. 'I only met the shell of a man, but he had a will of iron, I'm told.'

'And a heart of gold, or there wouldn't be so many here to see him off.'

Chris Santani caught up with them just as they were filing in, giving names to the reporter from the *Herald* at the church door. 'I went home to change, out of respect,' he explained. His tall frame was dressed in a dark three-piece suit. He was a very striking man. 'Poor Leo, a sad day for him. But he must be proud too.'

They shuffled into a pew. Dai said, 'I'd like to go like that—a totally fulfilled life, and then a quick death.'

'Quick?' Penny didn't ask how many years the old man had sat in that wheelchair. But she felt a great admiration for Leo, that he had kept his father at home. She felt a touch on her shoulder, and turned round to see Lil Donaldson behind her. Even Sam had made the effort, and sat beside her in his grey suit and black tie. 'Hello, Lil, Sam,' Penny greeted them.

Sam shook his head. 'Saw my old man out, he did. I won't be too far behind, I dare say. Good old man—I hope he leaves the pearly gates open for us.'

'Sam!' But Lil knew how bad her husband's heart condition was, and said no more.

The organists changed the melody. Chopin's Funeral March—grand and stately—reminding Penny suddenly of the Kremlin, and all the Russian funerals, with the row of men in hats on the wall by Lenin's tomb. This man they were mourning today was no dictator, but a much-loved physician.

Then silence. And another change of tune—a Handel organ concerto. Heads turned as the Vicar intoned the familiar words. The coffin came in, borne on the shoulders of grey-clad men, and the congregation stood up, with much rustling of silks and folding of programmes. Penny's eyes were riveted on the tall figure of Leo Zander, who walked alone behind the coffin. He was dressed in dark grey, with spotless white shirt and black silk tie. His dark head was slightly bent, his handsome eyes shadowed. She recalled his words—'I'm one of life's loners', and her heart went out to the dignified figure, and tears filled her eyes for Leo, not for Lionel. After him, in close formation, Janet Rhys-Evans walked with Mr and Mrs Banks. After them, a group of old and white-headed distinguished colleagues. Dai whispered the names of some of them—all respected in the field of medicine or science.

So Janet was next to Leo in importance. Penny knew how good she had been to the family, especially in the last years, so why was she irritated by Janet's comeliness? Black suited her, the neat pleated suit and the tasteful straw hat. She couldn't possibly be jealous? She squashed the idea, and concentrated on the first hymn.

One of the very old men in Leo's pew gave the address; Dai whispered that he was a professor at the University. He spoke of Lionel's long life, as a brilliant medical student, as an enthusiastic ship's doctor, and as a beloved GP. He added, in an aside, that the tradition was being admirably carried on by his only son. As he spoke Penny felt a sense of great pride flow over her. She was a part of this practice. She saw Chris Santani sit up straighter, and knew how he felt. That old, tumbledown Victorian surgery in James Street had been helping the community for as long as it had existed. They were a part of it, and it suddenly became something well worth being. She stole a sidelong look at Dai, and saw his jaw clench with a sudden emotion. Yes, it was a worthy partnership.

They filed out, to a great surge of Bach on the organ. Leo stood at the door, shaking hands. 'Come back to the house,' he smiled at his three partners. There was no sadness left now; the death of an old man with a happy life behind him was not an occasion for grief. Leo took Penny's hand and impulsively she reached up and kissed his cheek. His grip tightened and he looked down at her. 'You will come back, won't you?' he urged.

'Yes.'

'That's good.'

Leo's large house came to life. The dining room was laid with an elegant buffet. Mrs Banks and Janet presided while Mr Banks and one of the Banks daughters went round with trays of wine.

Penny found herself next to the Professor, and found that she was confiding how she had felt. He nodded in agreement. 'An old and proud tradition. James Street was once a street of the wealthy. It's come down in the world—but not, I'm happy to say, the standards of excellence practised there.'

Chris had joined them, and the Professor had been introduced, before being taken away by Janet to meet someone else. 'Excuse me, Penny dear, but Lady Taylor used to live next door to the Professor in Wallasey.'

'Of course,' smiled Penny.

Chris said, 'You get a sense of traditions, don't you? Today has made my mundane existence into something handed down, something valuable.'

Penny was glad that he felt it too. And glad that he had stopped his unwelcome personal attentions to her. Just then Joanie came up, her eyes red. 'I didn't see enough of him at the end. But he was always a good friend to Gemma and me,' she said.

'He had a happy life,' Penny reminded her.

'I know that, and I shouldn't be sad, but some people just matter more than others, don't they?'

Chris said, 'I know what you mean, Joanie. Can I get you another glass of wine?'

'No, thank you, Doctor. It'll make me even more weepy.'

She went across to talk to Leo. He put his hand on her shoulder in a friendly way, reminding Penny of the other night, when they had stood together looking at the view. And she suddenly recalled her dream of the ploughed field, of her struggle to reach the helping hand, the tall, comforting figure standing ready to help her if she could only get to him. She had thought it might have Robin White's face, but now she knew it was Leo who was standing holding out his hand to her. And she smiled to herself. What a fanciful dream! He would indeed help her—in exactly the same way as he helped Joanie, Janet,

Gemma, and anyone else who need him.

Lil Donaldson came up. 'Well, life will be different for Leo now,' she remarked.

Penny agreed. 'First he ought to take that Paris holiday.'

'So he ought, love. Janet's already been in touch with the travel agent about his flight, I believe.'

'Janet has?' Her heart felt like cement suddenly.

'She does so much for him—such a helpful soul! And so smart. I always said to Sam that he was lucky to have a neighbour like her.' She chuckled. 'Now a nice wedding is what this area needs next. What do you say, Penny?'

Penny smiled into the twinkling blue eyes. 'You think Leo and Janet . . . ?'

'Anything's possible. Now that his father has passed on—well, things might just move in that direction. You never know.'

Penny was remembering what Leo had said about marriage. It would have to be passionate, it had to be stormily vibrant, or he wanted nothing to do with it. He would never marry for convenience. Did he really regard Janet in that way? If only she could read him! But Leo was still able to cloak his real feelings with mystery —even to his closest associates. He could draw down the blinds on his secrets, and no one could penetrate to his heart.

She shook herself, reminding herself that in three months all this would be part of her past. She would have left Merseyside, left this practice. This warm feeling of belonging would have passed, and she would be a memory to them, as they would be a part of hers. It was no use regretting the decision. She knew it was the right one. She had learned a lot about medicine—a lot about life too, in all its variety. She would recall Liverpool with warmth as well as distaste for its blacker side, but it was not for her, and she would make it clear to Leo when they had to make the final decision in the new year.

Penny was off duty on the following Saturday. Joanie had made it clear that there were to be no church Christmas Fayres that weekend, and Penny had agreed with her. 'I'm going to curl up by the fire and catch up with the back numbers of the *British Medical Journal*,' she decided.

'I'm doing my Christmas card list.' Joanie was good at organising, making lists. 'Are you going to be with us for Christmas, Penny?'

'I think I'm going home to Brighton just for two days. I didn't manage it last year, and Mum and Dad were very disappointed.'

'Then I'll do you a turkey dinner before you go. Gemma will be disappointed if we don't.'

There was a ring at the bell, and Joanie put her ball pen behind her ear as she went to answer it. Penny heard female voices, then Joanie came back with Lalla Santani. 'Here's Mrs Santani, Penny, wanting a private word.'

Lalla was wearing a fur coat over a dark blue sari. 'Penny, I know I ought to see you in the surgery, but I did so want a private talk—while Chris is doing the Saturday surgery,' she added in a whisper.

'Come in, come in—of course it doesn't matter. You should have phoned me, Lalla. If you have any trouble, I'd have come round.'

'No—the children might have told Chris you were there.' She looked very apprehensive. 'I do not usually go against his wishes . . .'

'Tell me about it,' urged Penny.

'I want to go on the Pill,' Lalla burst out, 'but Chris will not hear of it.'

'I see. Do you take other precautions at present?'

'My husband does, but I do not trust it. My friend had twins when her husband was using precautions. I do not want any more children, Penny—I cannot stand any more headaches. I am sleeping alone now, and Chris is very angry with me—yet he refuses the Pill.'

'It's a common problem,' Penny told her. 'Some people fear its side effects. What about an IUCD? A device fitted into the womb?'

'That also he does not like. The doctors are men, and Indian men do not allow other men to touch their wives.'

'I can arrange it for you,' Penny told her. 'Look, let me tell you all the methods. You can think it over, and give me a call when you've decided. But don't sleep alone, Lalla. What's marriage if you're not loving together?'

'You are right. It makes me unhappy as well. But I am scared—I must not become pregnant again.' Lalla wiped the tears from her eyes with the corner of her sari. 'I am so unhappy, Penny, and I don't know why. I am angry with the children over little things—they make me very fed up. And then I quarrel with Chris too, about such small things that you would laugh at us for being so stupid.'

'It isn't a new problem, Lalla,' Penny assured her. 'Many English people have the same. What vitamins do you take?'

'None. I eat well, I think.'

'Would you mind if I took some blood to have tested? I think you might need some vitamins and iron to help you keep up with your lively kids.'

Lalla said quietly, 'I do not mind. I am grateful. But please do not tell Chris this is what we are doing—he will be so angry that I do not trust him completely. He will lose face, you see.'

'You have a right to look after your own health. I promise to say nothing.'

Lalla sighed. 'It was so different when we were in India.'

'You should have come to me earlier,' said Penny. 'But don't worry, I'm sure these two simple things will solve your problem—a reliable contraceptive and your own health building up.'

'Thank you,' smiled Lalla. 'I feel better now. Up till now I felt that I did nothing except drudge for other people. My husband—he brings home ten, twenty people, and expects me to cook. Okay, that I can do, if the children are not harassing me so much.'

'We'll soon have you fighting fit!' Penny told her.

The two women plotted together as to the next time they could meet, and when Penny could take some blood to be analysed. After Lalla had gone, she made a few notes to insert in Lalla's file when she went to the surgery on Monday. This interview with Lalla had gone a long way to explaining Chris's behaviour towards her. If the couple were sleeping apart, Chris would naturally be frustrated—a handsome and highly-sexed young man such as he. It did not excuse his advances, but it explained them somewhat. It was in Penny's interest as well as Lalla's to get Mrs Santani back into circulation. She was sure a tonic would help.

On Monday morning, Dai Richards' beloved Aston Martin was stolen. He had had a tiring weekend—with the lovely Andrea, presumably—and he came into the surgery tired and snappy. He swore that he had locked the car, but the police were sceptical. The surgery was crowded, too, as the first bouts of cold and 'flu began to take hold of the population. The decorators were in, trying to finish the papering. And in the midst of the mêlée, Kay came out of the office to tell them that Judy was having hysterics in the loo.

Leo separated the combatants, and sent Dai to his room with the police officers. He asked the decorators to take a tea break, and he took Judy into Penny's consulting room, which was less noisy, first asking the milling crowd in the waiting room to be as patient as possible. They listened to Leo—didn't everyone? But naturally the crying children could not be quieted.

Leo sat in Penny's chair, while she patted Judy's shaking shoulders. Kay stood at the door, looking daggers. Leo said, 'Now, tell me the trouble, Judy. I've got all the time in the world. Let's hear it.'

Between sobs, it became clear that Judy's son had been caught by the police in possession of heroin, and brought home in a panda car, in full view of the neighbours. 'He's only fourteen. If he's started so young, there'll be no stopping him!' she sobbed.

Kay said sourly, 'If she's that upset, she'd better go home, Doctor. Surgery's too busy for this pantomime.'

Leo said quietly, 'Bring her a cup of tea, Kay. Penny, any Valium?'

Penny handed one over, and Leo waited until Judy had quietened down. 'Right. Now, if you can, go back to work, and care for these people's problems. We'll have a proper chat at the end of the surgery.' He stood up to go back to his room.

Kay said, 'If we ever finish. The queue is out of the door.'

Penny resumed her chair. 'Go and start, Kay. Judy will come along in just a minute. Get them in an orderly line, and send me the first patient,' she directed.

Kay nodded. 'But don't buzz at me, Doctor, or I'll have a nervous breakdown!'

'All right, Kay, I won't buzz,' Penny promised.

It was after two when the four doctors finished surgery. They handed out the calls glumly. Kay had made coffee, but told them there was no sugar and she had no time to get any. She slammed the call book down.

Suddenly there was an almighty crash from the upstairs office, where the decorators stored their ladders, and Leo looked heavenwards. 'I hope no one has damaged anything worse than a ladder. It wasn't a thunderbolt, was it?'

'Losing an expensive car and being arrested for drug possession are enough thunderbolts for one morning!'

Penny waited for her call list, trying not to be appalled at the length of it.

Dai picked up his. 'I'll take a taxi,' he said stonily. He was on the defensive, because of still owing the surgery money for the car, although nobody was heartless enough to remind him.

Leo called after him, 'Take a half-day, Dai.'

Dai turned at the door. 'No, sir! No half-days during epidemics. I may be a fool about money, but I won't leave you to manage short-staffed.'

Leo's face betrayed signs of stress for the first time. He was leafing through the pile of letters again, not finding the one he wanted. 'Penny, they haven't written about Gordon Williams' operation, have they?'

'No. The boys say he's okay.'

'I'd rather speak to the registrar, but there isn't time.'

Penny said calmly, 'We can do it later in the week.'

He snapped suddenly, 'You're in charge now, then?'

She didn't quail. 'Just an idea that would help.'

'Hmm.' Leo looked up at her then, and his stern look softened. He stood up. 'Right, let's get started. Don't breathe any germs. 'And make sure you have a couple of disposable masks with you—we can't afford to lose anyone with 'flu ourselves.'

Leo had gone. Penny went back to her room, slipped off her white coat, and put on her sheepskin jacket. Chris Santani came in; she thought she was the last to leave. She looked up at the tall figure and saw that his handsome face was thunderous. 'Penny, I'd be glad if you would stay away from my wife!' he snapped furiously.

She had admitted it, then. 'She needed advice,' Penny told him calmly.

'I am perfectly capable of looking after my own family!' The usually polite voice was raised with anger. He caught Penny's arm roughly. 'You are interfering in my house, and I do not allow that!'

'Chris, she's tired and sad. Have you thought of testing for anaemia?'

'Clinically she is not anaemic. She complains a lot, but that is her nature.'

'Chris, I've got work to do.' Penny tried to open the door, but Chris put his foot against it. Then he stood with his back to it and pulled her roughly into his arms, kissing her mouth, and sliding his hands under her coat, so that he could caress her body.

She realised they were alone. The others had all gone. The phone was on transfer and the door was locked. Penny tried not to panic. Summoning all her strength, she ducked suddenly, escaped from his grip, leaving her coat in his arms, and ran to put her desk between them. From that place of safety, she let fly in her fiercest voice. 'You prove my point, Chris. You can act like a brute —to me and to the wife who loves you. You're frustrated, Chris—and instead of putting things right with Lalla, you try to take it out on me!'

Chris stood staring at her, breathing hard, his black eyes sharp with anger. Then he placed her coat slowly on the desk. 'Stay away from my affairs, Dr Harcourt. I'll see my solicitor about this!' And he opened the door with one angry twist, and strode out.

Penny followed, after she had combed her hair and refastened her coat, waiting for her heartbeats to return to normal. She was just walking to the outside door when there was a sound of breaking glass, and a brick landed on the waiting room floor. Bits of glass lay all over the floor, and through the jagged hole came the sound of young lads giggling as they ran away along the windy street.

CHAPTER TEN

The Christmas decorations went up in the city of Liverpool. Children asked happily for computer games and electronic marvels, and parents tried to direct their attentions away from the costly advertisements. But at the surgery at Number 7 James Street, the 'flu epidemic went on, and the spirit of Christmas was nowhere to be seen. True, Kay had put up a small artificial tree, but a naughty child with a harassed mother had pulled it to the ground and smashed the baubles. And somehow it looked pathetic in its new position high on a bracket where children could not reach it—but no one could see it either.

The four doctors hardly exchanged two words that were not business, as they worked together to contain the epidemic. Like robots they came to work each morning. The one who had been on call had the blackest rings around his eyes. Even Penny, who was the youngest, looked tired, her skin had lost its bloom, and her hair was lank with neglect. When she was off duty she spent the time asleep. When she was on, she refused any offers of help. She preferred to pull her weight equally, and she did it.

She was proud and independent. And she was also determined not to be browbeaten by Chris Santani. She took a sample of blood from Lalla, had it tested at the hospital lab, and gave Lalla the necessary vitamins and iron that she needed. It was not underhand—it was vital for the woman, who in turn was responsible for the health of the whole family. Penny was not a girl to hold back when there was something that needed doing.

At the end of the third week of December, the partners found themselves finishing surgery with time to spare. They met in Leo's room to drink their coffee, but there was little chat. Everyone was wrapped up in their own weariness, their own problems. Leo laid down the last letter of the pile he had read. 'Well, things seem quieter. Perhaps we should talk about organising a Christmas party?'

Dai said immediately, 'Count me out, Leo. I'm not in a festive mood.'

'That goes for me too. My wife is giving me hell.' Chris turned away.

Penny couldn't let that go. 'And whose fault is that?' she demanded.

'Probably yours,' he snapped back.

Judy came over to pick up Leo's letters. 'I'm not in a party mood,' she sighed. 'Trevor's case comes up in the beginning of the new year.'

Kay was sour and cynical. 'And I've just about had enough of this madhouse! I need a break. I've seen enough patients, police and workmen to last me a lifetime. When we'll get some normality God only knows.'

Leo was impassive. 'The general opinion is that we don't bother with a party this year. Very well, subject closed.'

The others left with murmurs of farewell, but Leo called Penny back. 'You didn't mind? Not having a surgery get-together?'

She laughed without amusement. 'It wouldn't have been a load of laughs. No one is in the right mood.'

'How about you?' he queried.

'I'll be going home for a day or two.'

He smiled. 'I hope you enjoy it, away from all our wrangling! But it isn't always like this, you know.' He put a hand gently on her shoulder as she turned to go. 'I hope you have a happy time, anyway.'

'I hope you do.' Of course he would. He would have Janet, wouldn't he?

'I was going to ask you to my house for Christmas Day,' Leo added.

She would not have enjoyed being condescended to by Janet. 'That's very decent of you,' she said.

'Maybe next year?' His eyes were unreadable again.

'Leo!' Penny protested.

'I'm serious,' he told her.

'I'm not likely to be living very near here,' she reminded him.

'Oh no—I'd forgotten.'

'You had not.'

'Maybe not. You might have changed your mind, though—it's not too late. Have you looked for another place yet?'

'Not yet. But I'm keeping an eye on the vacancies.'

He said slowly, 'If I can't find anyone, would you consider doing a locum?'

'I would, of course. Depending on my next job.'

'Thanks. You'll be looking for somewhere in the south, I suppose?'

'Yes,' said Penny.

'Pity. You'll find it tame—no guts needed, no character, no challenge. You're the kind of person who needs to be stretched. You'd die of boredom if you went south.'

She turned to look into his face, her feelings touched. He was trying very hard to persuade her to stay, so he must want her quite a lot. And if it were just the work, she might have at least put off her departure. But it was the personal things that she could not bear—not least the coolness between the partners. And the way Leo Zander was dominated by one woman. A man like him—Penny turned away again without speaking. As she went to the door, she said, the words wrenched out of her by his unaccustomed silence, 'I'll miss you.'

'Penny——' She turned again, faced him, and the challenge in those brown eyes. They were so gentle now. 'Have a wonderful Christmas. And let me know when your train gets in, I'll meet you at Lime Street.'

'Are you sure? Thanks, Leo,' she smiled.

It was dark outside and there was a touch of frost in the air. The lamp-post outside the door was glistening, and the circle of light beneath it. The others had gone, and James Street was very quiet. The warehouses were bolted and dead, the curtains in the terraced houses were drawn tight, like tightly closed eyes. There was no traffic, only the two cars parked at the kerbside. A brief burst of laughter came from the pub across the road, and a distant chorus of 'Good King Wenceslas'.

Leo turned towards his car, key in hand, and Penny watched him silhouetted against the yellow street light. She had a sudden feeling, like in her dream, that she might never see him again. 'Leo—' she began.

He turned, and half held out his arms, and Penny found herself deep in his embrace, her cheek against the roughness of his overcoat, clinging to him desperately, as though she couldn't bear to leave him. He held her close, kissing her hair, caressing it with his fingers, pressing her to him as though she were very precious indeed. 'Penny, sweet Penny—' he muttered.

'Don't go yet.' Surely she hadn't said those words? She had only thought them, as they surged up from her subconscious. Penny wasn't sure about anything any more. But Leo's embrace was strong and lasting, in that chill deserted street. She lost count of time, as they stood close together, not wanting to break the spell, knowing that in this place she felt totally and completely happy.

His words were half hidden by her hair. 'Happy Christmas, darling.' And he bent and kissed her lips, a lingering sweet kiss that she returned with abandon.

Had he really called her darling? Her imagination was playing tricks. It had sounded so right, so lovely . . .

'And to you, Leo. Good night.' She moved slightly away, but he pulled her back for one last, brief kiss. She broke away then, and almost ran to her little car.

Leo stood where she had left him. 'And don't forget to ring!' he called.

'Yes, I'll ring. Good night!'

She started the engine with a nervous twist of the key. 'Start, damn you!' she muttered. She felt as though she had betrayed far too much of herself to Leo. She wanted to hide—but she knew her hands were trembling, and she ought not to drive yet. It didn't occur to her that he had shown too much of himself to her—poor Penny was unversed in love, and she fought shy of allowing the word to swim into her mind.

As she parked the car in the yard, Patrick O'Hare was coming down the steps from Joanie's flat. He must have been for a Christmas drink. That was nice. He was a jolly man, got on well with everyone—especially Joanie . . . 'Hello, my dear,' he greeted Penny. 'It's a happy family reunion they've got up there.'

'Hi, Patrick. Is Gemma back already?'

'She is—and in very good spirits.'

'Good. All the best, Patrick,' she smiled.

'Have a wonderful, blessed time, Penny my dear.'

She went up the steps, after waving goodbye to Patrick. She reached in her bag for the latchkey, but before she found it, Gemma had thrown open the door. She threw herself into Penny's arms. 'Penny, Penny, how lovely to see you! I'm home for good, Penny. Happy Christmas, and how I wish you were having it with us—I'm going to miss you so very much!'

Penny put her arms round the excited girl, as they walked in together. Joanie was in the kitchen, her face bright, her tired eyes animated and sparkling. 'Isn't it great? She came home a day early!' she smiled.

'She looks wonderful,' Penny agreed. 'And I'll only be away a couple of nights, Gemma. I'll be back to take you to a show after Christmas. And I'll expect you to take me to the January sales—I need lots of new clothes!'

It was taken for granted that Penny stayed in the kitchen with them, that they set the table for three, and that Jade considered her knee totally agreeable for curling up on. Gemma sat beside her, chattering about the last days at school, and how nice everyone was now that she was leaving. Even Miss Dartford had wished her luck and a happy Christmas.

As the London train slid out of Lime Street next day, crowded with others going home for Christmas, Penny felt a tug at her heart, and knew she was sorry to be leaving Merseyside. The street lights were on, the shops brightly decorated. True, the Regent Street lights in London would be grander, but Penny had been among these people. Pour and run-down as the city was, it was rich in spirit, in gaiety and optimism. It refused to admit defeat—like Joanie, and Tim Watson, and Lil Donaldson, and Debbie Grant. Penny's mind flitted from one to the other. Not only patients—friends who she had become fond of. In her bag was a parcel of Christmas cards from all of them. She took them out, read the messages of love and gratitude. There were tears on her cheeks, and she was suddenly homesick for dirty old James Street—even for dapper young Chris, for gruff Dai, for Father, the one who made everything all right . . .

By the time she had changed trains, and stood up half the way to Brighton, Penny's thoughts had made the transition. She now looked forward, not back. Mum and Dad would have aged since she saw them last summer. The little bungalow would be the same, the single bed she had had since a child, and the pictures on the walls—a Dégas ballet dancer, and a copy of *The Hay Wain*.

The welcome was as warm as always. The little house was decorated, the tree was in the corner of the parlour, and there was a delicious smell of cooking. 'Mum, I've dreamed of your casseroles!' laughed Penny.

'You've gone thin, Penny,' her mother fretted. 'You were always such a bonny girl. Look at that dress—it's hanging on you!'

'Thinner but fitter, Mum. How about you? You've put on a bit.'

'We both have. Your dad can't take as much exercise as he used to.'

'Then you should give him less to eat—more fruit.'

'Don't lecture us as soon as you get through the door, Penny!' scolded her father.

'Sorry, Dad.'

'You're to sit down and let yourself be spoiled a bit,' her mother said firmly. 'You must have been worked to death, to lose that weight. Come and have a bit of decent dinner, and tell us all about Liverpool.'

'Well, first, I'm not worked to death, and my land-lady is a poppet, and a marvellous cook,' Penny told them.

'Do they want you to stay?' Her mother's face was round and rosy, her wispy white hair framing it with silver.

Penny said, 'Let's not talk about it tonight.' The memory of her last conversation with Leo was still sharp in her mind, and for a moment she saw him again in her mind's eye, outlined against the street light, saw him open his arms and take her to him as though she belonged. That frosty street was real—it was this cosy little bungalow that was only a mirage . . .

It was dark, but the curtains were still open. Outside, her father's neat little garden, and the sound of the sea. 'It reminds me of my flat. I can hear the Mersey from my room,' she said.

'The Mersey? It must be filthy,' commented her mother.

'No, Mum, they sit along the prom and catch fish. The

sand is sand-coloured. The grass is green. And the sunsets are out of this world. From my senior partner's window . . .'

Her father shook his head. 'Sunsets are one thing, unemployment and vandalism are quite another.'

'It's when unemployment is high that they need good doctors, Dad.' Penny leaned across the table, tapping it to make her point. 'There are so many illnesses caused by loneliness and inadequacy, and you can help them so much if you understand them . . .' she broke off, remembering what Leo had said to her. She was copying his prediction—that she needed a challenge. She hid a smile. Was Leo Zander some sort of Svengali, influencing her very thoughts?

Her mother smiled as she cleared the table. 'You are staying on, then.'

'Nothing's decided yet.'

'Well, shall we put the telly on? There's a good film, and the Christmas editions of some of the comedy shows.'

'Yes, come on. I haven't sat and frowsted in front of the telly for months!' Penny settled back against the cushion—and suddenly missed Jade's furry presence, and the heavy affection of Bathsheba sending her feet to sleep . . .

She slept well, tired out, for the first half of the night, but she woke very early on Christmas morning, feeling very strange, very far away from the north-west of the country. Yet she wouldn't be missed. They all had their own friends, their own families . . . She didn't really fit in; she was only a temporary Liverpudlian. They would soon welcome a new doctor, and she would not be missed.

But as she read through the cards once again, before her parents got up, she was again influenced by their warmth, their gratitude. Leo was quite right: Liverpool had brought out the best in her. And it had rewarded her, too, with the approval and love of these worthy people.

If only the surgery colleagues hadn't had so many disagreements! She was fond of them, but their last meeting had been rather dismal. Chris was in all probability not speaking to her, Dai was wrapped up in his affairs, Kay and Judy were depressed. And Leo was getting ready to fly to Paris to see a long-standing friend—one of many.

Her mother had knitted her a jumper and her father had bought her a book token. She gave them a hamper of goodies, including caviare, pâté and champagne. Penny managed to forget Liverpool, as they unwrapped their presents, and talked of friends and relatives they must call on before she went back. The smell of the roasting turkey wafted in, getting more and more tempting. Nobody in the world cooked a turkey like Mum!

And then the telephone rang. Penny shot across the room to pick up the receiver, as though someone had stuck a pin in her—and as she heard Leo's voice, she knew why. 'Is that you, Penny?' he asked.

'It is. Happy Christmas, Leo.' She couldn't disguise the warmth in her voice. It was so sweet of him to call.

'All the very best, my dear. Gemma refused to eat until we'd spoken to you,' he laughed.

So Leo hadn't thought of it. Disappointment flooded over her and the pleasure in the call vanished. She had wanted Leo to miss her, not Gemma. 'Hello, Gemma my darling,' she greeted the girl. 'Have a wonderful day.'

'Thank you so terribly much for the gorgeous leotard!' said Gemma excitedly. 'It's the best I've ever seen!'

'I'm sure you look dishy in it,' Penny told her.

'Wish you were here, Penny!' sighed Gemma.

'See you the day after tomorrow.'

'Okay. Have a nice Christmas dinner.'

Then Joanie's voice. 'Happy day, Penny. Give my love to your folks.'

'Happy Christmas, Joanie.'

And then the voice she had hoped she wouldn't hear. 'Penny? Janet here. Greetings and all good wishes, my dear.'

'And to you. I'm sure you'll all have a wonderful time.'

'It would have been nice if you were here too,' Janet added.

'Janet, how nice of you! You make it sound as though I belong.'

'Well, my dear, you are always around, aren't you? I'd got quite used to you as one of our regulars.'

Leo came on. 'Penny, we have to go. I'm taking them to a hotel.' He had taken over before Janet's good wishes became too frigid. 'Did you check on your return train?'

'Yes. I'll be in Lime Street at four,' Penny told him.

'I'll be there.'

'Thanks. Goodbye.'

'God bless you, Penny.' He replaced the receiver. Penny held it for a while, listening to the tone, and imagining them all piling out to squeeze into the Rover. His voice had deepened to its dark brown velvet colour. It touched her suddenly, and she found two tears already rolling down her cheeks, before she took control of herself and put the phone down briskly. 'Just my boss and his house party,' she told her parents.

'That sounds grand,' her father commented.

Grand? Not Leo, he wasn't like that. 'No, Dad,' she assured him.

'What's he like?' asked her mother.

'Just about impossible—to describe, I mean. He's—well, good-looking, kind, strict——'

'And his wife?'

'He isn't married.'

'Engaged?'

'Possibly having an affair with the next-door neighbour,' shrugged Penny.

'Really? Is she nice too?'

Penny laughed. 'Dad, forget him! He's a strange man—distant, yet magnetic.'

'You sound as though you're one of the bits of metal he's attracted.'

'I like him. He's a good teacher,' she said evasively.

'I can see that,' said her mother drily.

'Mum, what does that look mean?' demanded Penny.

'I saw such a nice suit the other day, wondered whether to buy it and keep it on one side.'

'Mother!' she protested. 'You aren't going to be mother of the bride yet! I want to establish my career first. There's lots of time for marriage after that.'

'Yes, dear. Are we having your champagne? I did put it in the fridge.'

'Right, I'll get the glasses.' They set the table together, and no more was said about Leo Zander.

The meal was good. The toast was from her father. 'To the best Christmas we've had for two years.'

'Dad, I'm sorry,' Penny apologised. 'I'll do my best to make it next year.'

But she felt restless. And Boxing Day was tedious, as they made the rounds of old family friends. She looked at her watch, counting the hours until the train arrived in Lime Street on the twenty-seventh of December at four in the afternoon.

Her father sat with her as she looked out of the window for the taxi. 'Dr Johnson said the finest view a Scotsman sees is the high road that takes him to England,' he remarked.

'I know.' Penny smiled at him. 'What are you getting at?'

'It seems that the finest sight to my daughter is the taxi

that takes her part of the way back to Liverpool,' he said ruefully.

Penny shook her head. 'It's nothing like that, Dad. I just don't want to miss the train—it would be awkward for Leo.'

'Oh, so he's coming to meet you?'

'Don't read into things! He's just a kind man—I told you he was.'

'And you're a very pretty girl. Even kind men have eyes in their heads.'

Penny said nothing. She must be very naïve if they saw how her thoughts clung to the memory of Leo. Just then the taxi drew up, and there was only time for a hug and a kiss. 'Don't worry, I've given my notice. I'll be back in a couple of months,' she told her father.

'We'll look forward to it.'

'Goodbye, goodbye!'

In the train she tried to be logical. Only two more months: she could surely live through that without any further trauma. She would be businesslike and busy. She would be affable without being over-friendly. Not that Chris Santani would be friendly, but he seemed to have dropped his threat of bringing the law into matters. She was going back to a litter-strewn city, where so soon the lights would be going out, and the streets return to being their usual drab wasteland of hopelessness and despair. In another day or so the festive season would have finished, and people begin to face reality again. Just as Penny had to do.

But now Lime Street was near, and in spite of her resolve, she felt her heartbeats quicken. The train jerked forward, halted, and jerked again. She stood up to get her small suitcase from the rack, her cheeks pink at the thought of the man who was waiting for her on the station. When Leo was there, it was hard to see Liverpool as anything but the best place in the world to be.

The train was crowded and it took quite some time for Penny to get off, to make the trek from her coach at the back of the train, all along the platform to the ticket barrier. It was a cold frosty afternoon and her fingers were cold as she gripped her case in one hand, and her ticket in the other. She began to imagine being whisked off in the Rover, back to warmth and friendship, to Joanie and Gemma. And to Leo's gentle presence, making all things right.

He wasn't on the station. He wasn't by the barrier. Of course—it was hard to get a parking place. He would be waiting in the car park by his car, standing up, looking out for her. Penny hurried up, stumbling a bit past the slower walkers all making for the exit, for the taxi rank.

She reached the car park, looked round for his dark Rover. He must be here—how could Leo ever let her down? She even now began to imagine the slow smile, the way the dark eyes would brighten as he spotted her, his firm warm handshake as he took the case from her, and opened the car door.

'Yoo-hoo! Penny, yoo-hoo!'

She turned, looked all round. It was a woman's voice. The car park was very crowded. Then she saw a hand waving—yes, it was Leo's car. With light steps, she waved back, then picked up her case and hurried across towards the Rover.

Her heart fluttering, she said, 'Hello, Janet,' and looked into the car. Janet was alone.

'Welcome home, Penny. Sorry I couldn't leave the car, but I'm on a yellow line. Did you have a good time? Parents well?'

'Yes, thanks.'

'We had a fabulous time, the best ever.' Janet opened the doors, and eased herself behind the driving wheel. 'Leo is such good company. Poor darling, he missed his father a little. But he's going to be able to relax and enjoy life a bit more now.'

'He's all right, is he?' asked Penny.

'Couldn't be better.'

'Only—you having the car . . . ?'

'Mine wouldn't start,' Janet explained. 'He isn't on call, so he lent me the Rover for the day. Mr Banks is looking under my bonnet for me this afternoon.'

It all sounded so normal. They might almost have been a married couple already. Her car wouldn't start, so she borrows his. Penny choked back the one question she dearly wanted to ask: why didn't he come himself? It was obvious, really—he didn't think it mattered. Janet was in the driving seat in more senses than one. Janet was his right hand, his second in command, his protector and loyal slave. Janet would do to collect that rather tiresome junior assistant of his.

How on earth could she have imagined anything else? That she, a mousy assistant, could have crept anywhere near his heart, even a tiny bit. The tall, aloof Leo, the dashing, self-sufficient Leo—how foolish she was to interpret his kindness as anything more than a fatherly appreciation for her loyalty and hard work.

Now at least, by sending Janet, he had set the record absolutely clear. Now she saw things straight; it was obvious. 'Well, thanks for coming for me, Janet,' she said flatly. 'It was very kind of you.'

'Not at all, dear. I had to come into town to get the tickets. The travel agent was keeping them for me.'

CHAPTER ELEVEN

THE drizzle had turned to sleet as Penny drove in for morning surgery next day. Even with the wipers full on, the windscreen was getting sheeted over with white. She drove carefully, applying the brakes sparingly, keeping a good length away from the car in front at the round-about. She parked in her usual place. It was good that she had something to worry about; it would keep her mind from dwelling on things that upset her.

She went into the hall, stamping the slush from her boots and knocking the white flakes from her hair. Kay came out of the office, looking spruce in a new white coat. 'Good morning, Doctor.' The greeting almost sang along the corridor.

'Hello, Kay. You sound cheerful,' Penny remarked.

'I'm feeling great!' smiled Kay.

'You had a nice Christmas?'

'Yes, lovely. But it's more than that. I really feel well. I think those tablets you gave me are working.'

'At last! I knew you needed some type of hormone replacement, but it was just a question of getting the dosage right.' Penny went along to her room. Kay's obvious good humour had lifted her mood one notch. Kay was quick to follow her with a cup of tea. 'That's a kind thought, Kay.'

'Well, a nice cuppa helps, on a rotten day like this.'

'Waiting room seems quiet,' Penny remarked.

'There won't be many until after New Year, only the regulars for repeat prescriptions.' Kay was ready to chat this morning. 'Have you seen the waiting room? The men came and finished it off yesterday, and it looks really great.' And Penny had to take a peep at the newly

157

painted room. The Christmas tree had been taken down, re-ornamented, and put back on the mantelpiece. Kay turned and smiled at Penny. 'Don't you think good working conditions make for a contented staff? I was gloomy before—because the room was grotty.'

'And you hadn't responded to your hormone replacement therapy.'

'That as well,' laughed Kay.

'What about me?' queried Penny. 'Have you ever tried to work in a wardrobe?'

Kay grinned again. 'But you aren't the complaining type, Doctor. I'm good at it!'

'Well, I must say it's a joy to hear you make a joke about it.' Penny sat back in her chair, and checked the morning mail—one or two late Christmas cards, and some hospital letters. One of the cards had a picture of Magdalen College, Oxford, and inside, 'With very best wishes, Robin and Ann White.' She hadn't sent them a card. She must call and thank them. The thought of Robin didn't hurt at all now; she had learned the hard way not to be too gullible. She would call—when the weather improved.

The phone went. Kay said, 'Doctor, there's a call from Tim Watson's daughter in Wales.'

'Put her through.' There had been a letter about Tim in the day's post. 'Dr Harcourt here.'

'Me mum's asked me to come home, Doctor. Does that mean me dad's bad?' The voice sounded pathetically young and tearful. 'Only I've got the baby, and he's only two months, and I'll come if I'm needed, but I'll have to come alone because me husband can't get time off, 'cos he'll be made redundant . . .'

'Your father's in intensive care, but he's not dying,' Penny told her. 'His condition is stable, and the hospital say there's no danger.'

Poor man! If only he had been the complaining type. On the other hand, perhaps Penny ought to have spotted his trouble earlier . . . 'Me mum sounded worried,' the voice went on.

'Naturally. It was a shock to her—your father was such a cheerful man. But no, there's no need. I'll take your number, and let you know at once if there's any need.'

'Thank you. Thank you very much!'

Kay was right about the regulars. Penny found herself smiling as they trooped in, one by one. She knew them all, was familiar with their problems, even remembered their blood pressures, and when they last went to clinic. This was general practice—mundane, perhaps, routine, sometimes. But mainly it was being accepted as a trusted member of the family, knowing all their secrets, familiar with their in-laws—and most of all, being welcomed with a smile.

'Your chest is very much clearer, Mr Eaton,' she told one man.

'I've you to thank for that, lass. Dr Zander couldn't get me off the fags. It was the way you explained it to me—you really put me off!'

'And you feel better?'

'Better than I've felt for years. I didn't even get the 'flu. The missus got it, and she's never smoked in her life.' He chuckled, then coughed. Years of smoking had indeed taken their toll. If he was lucky, he'd get away with simple bronchitis, now that he'd given up.

'I feel we ought to have a medal for people like you, Mr Eaton. I'm really proud of you,' Penny told him.

'We're proud of you, lass. You've done a lot of good here. I didn't want a lady doctor, I'll tell you straight. When you first come, I didn't want to know. But you're a right good lass.' He picked up his cap. 'And thank you again.'

'Wrap up well in this weather, and don't take any chances,' she warned.

'Aye, I will.'

She watched him go. His back was straighter, now that that hacking cough had left him. She was smiling as she pressed the buzzer for the next patient. It was good to be back among friends.

But after surgery, as she went towards Leo's room, where Kay had taken the coffee, Penny hesitated slightly. How did one face a man who sent his girl-friend to meet one? And was it possible to speak naturally to him, after that impassioned embrace they had shared the night before she went to Brighton? She pushed open the door. She was the first; Leo was alone. He looked up from his desk, where he sat, his handsome head bent over some letters he was signing, then he stood up as she hovered on the threshold, and came towards her. She didn't look into his face. She must be distant now; he had made it clear. 'You had a good holiday?' he asked.

'Yes, very good.' Silence. They both stood, close but not touching. Penny said, 'It was generous of Mrs Rhys-Evans to meet me.'

'She insisted. She had some shopping to do, and some tickets to get.' He shrugged, as though he knew the excuse was lame. 'I couldn't insist on going with her—it looked unnecessary for two of us to make the trip.'

'I do see.' Janet had been picking up the tickets for the two of them to go to Paris, then. Penny went across to the window, turning her back on him.

Leo went back to his desk. 'There are some trouble-some calls this morning.' His voice was cold, impersonal. 'I won't ask you to go to the Dorlings. Three of the kids have coughs, one has measles, and both the parents have hangovers.'

Penny said calmly, 'I've been before. You can give them to me if you like.'

'No, it's Dai's turn. He had it easy, being off on Christmas Day.'

She said sharply, 'There's no need to punish him for that! Or is that your sense of duty again?'

'Fairness, Penny.' His tone was mild. 'I don't inflict my sense of duty on others, do I?'

Before she could think of a reply, Chris and Dai came in together, laughing heartily about some private joke. Dai hooted at the sight of Penny. 'You've come back to us, Penny! Welcome home.'

'Thanks, Dai.' She turned to smile at him. 'It's nice to see you cheerful again.'

'We Welsh are incapable of gloom for more than three weeks at a stretch,' he joked. 'My natural optimism breaks through after that.'

Leo said drily, 'Then perhaps you won't mind seeing the Dorling family? I would imagine all the children are sickening for measles, as one has it, but we'd better make sure.'

Dai nodded, unperturbed. 'Sure, I'll visit the little darlings. No doubt Father is still celebrating Christmas?'

'No doubt. Don't antagonise him again, will you?'

'Me? have no fear. The famous Richards tact will be brought into play.'

Leo ticked off his calls and passed the book to Chris. Chris checked his list. 'You want to see Gordon Williams, Penny?'

'Yes, of course.'

Leo said, 'Give them my best. That family have had a terrible year. Let's hope the new year is kinder to them.'

Penny said, 'You had a letter from the hospital?'

'Yes. Operation a complete success.'

'Right.'

Chris made out his list. 'Right, I'll push off if you don't want me, I told Lalla I'd probably be early.'

Dai laughed. 'Hey, Chris, no drug lunches? This can't be Dr Santani actually going home?'

Chris took the laughter with a superior smile. 'Poor Dai. Never mind, one day your fairy godmother might find you a lovely wife and family—if you're very good and don't antagonise Mr Dorling.'

Penny was excited. So Chris was going home to his family! Her therapy must be working. She looked slyly at Chris, but his face was open and natural, sharing the joke with Dai, but eager to be off.

Leo said from his desk, 'Do you think that fairy godmother would do something for me too, Chris, while she's at it?'

'Come on, Father! You only have to snap your fingers and half the housewives in Liverpool rush to scrub your toenails, man.' Dai sounded envious. Penny kept her eyes on the floor. They all laughed, but the telephone interrupted the jollity.

'Zander?' He listened for a moment. 'All right, I'll tell Penny.' He put the receiver down. 'That was Joanie. Gemma's been brought home from a pub—she's been drinking. She's home now, and Joanie wants your advice.'

'I'll make it in about an hour.' Penny went to the door at once. 'But she mustn't keep relying on me. She's going to have to be a full-time mum soon.'

'I'm sure we all know that you're leaving soon enough.' Leo's tone was harsh, as he turned again to his lists. 'But give her a hand while you're here. You've been a great help so far.' Penny nodded and went out. There it was again, the special relationship between Leo and Joanie. What was the tie between them? She closed the door behind her, trying not to let it worry her.

Her final call was just to see Gordon Williams. He had been discharged from hospital on anti-convulsant drugs, and would need a further prescription. He was cheerful and looked well, though he wore a woolly cap to hide his shaved head. 'I'm bored, Doctor,' he complained. 'In the shop, Christmas and New Year was the busiest time —everyone having their hair done for parties and balls and that. We were worked off our feet, from nine in the morning to after eight at night. It was fun, though.'

'Is there nothing you can do at home?' Penny asked.

'I've got an old typewriter—thought maybe I'd write a short story about my experiences.'

'Good idea. Send it to Radio Merseyside,' she suggested.

'Hey, me on radio—that's not a bad idea!'

'Better than TV, with a hairstyle like yours,' she smiled.

'Yes, total baldness isn't really the style for a hairdresser. It might catch on.' Gordon was certainly very well in himself, no sign of the irritation and ill feeling that had persisted before operation. He came with her to the door. 'We'll miss you, Dr Harcourt. You've been good news for our family. It'll be like losing me mam again.'

Touched, she said, 'You'll be fit by then, Gordon. You probably won't need a doctor ever again.' All the same, as she turned and waved, she knew she would miss the little family in Davies Road.

She sat in the car, ready to turn its nose towards home. Gemma was waiting for her ticking off. What had made her go into a pub? She must have been with a crowd, and not been willing to say no when they all went in.

But as she passed St Edmund's Vicarage, Penny decided to get her duty call of thanks over. She rang the bell.

'How lovely to see you! Please come in—Robin is sick visiting again.' Ann White was alone. The baby was crawling about round her feet, and the older boy was home from school, bouncing a very new football in the Vicarage hall.

'Just for a moment,' said Penny. 'I came to say thank you for the card. It was lovely.'

'Robin's idea. He's very fond of you, you know.' Ann said it artlessly; there was no suggestion of anything more than friendship.

Penny said sincerely, 'He did help me a lot—to come to terms with the awfulness of some people's lives.'

'Yes, I'm sure he did. Robin's like that, so genuinely Christian about everything. I feel an awful fraud alongside his idealism.'

Penny said impulsively, 'You must come along and meet Joanie and Gemma one of these days.' She liked Ann's frank and open manner. It was silly to stay away from the Whites just because she once had a fanciful idea about Robin. That was all over now. And Ann was clearly delighted to be invited.

'I find myself going up the wall sometimes for the need of someone sane to talk to. Robin is a darling, but he's never here. I'm terribly behind with the magazine at the moment—as the only typist in the parish, I've got it all to do.'

'I say!' Penny was suddenly struck with an idea. 'I say, this may not work, but I've just been talking to a man with a typewriter and not enough to do.'

'Tell me more,' Ann invited.

Penny proceeded to tell. She left Ann White in a state of happy anticipation that at last she might have a helping hand. 'Give me a ring if it works out,' she told her.

'Thanks, Penny. Happy New Year!'

Penny drove back, thinking again how friends made a place good to be in. It seemed pretty obvious that it was the people you share your life with who make it worthwhile—not some picture-book prettiness of surroundings. She ought perhaps to hesitate before cutting herself off from Merseyside—at least tell Leo that she would like a chance to think it over. She would do that, next time she found herself alone with him.

She opened the flat door quietly, but Gemma was waiting for her, and she rushed to meet her before she had time to close the door. 'Penny, Penny, I'm most terribly sorry for upsetting Mum! I knew I shouldn't have gone to the pub, honest, but I did so want to stay with the gang.'

Penny couldn't help it; she put her arms round Gemma and hugged her. 'Darling, I'm hungry and tired. If you'll bring me a large mug of hot tea, we'll go to my room and have a nice long talk.'

'I'll do better than that. I've made you some cheese and bacon sandwiches. I'll toast them for you while I make the tea.' And in a few minutes Gemma came in with Penny's lunch, savoury and very welcome to the tired girl.

Penny noticed that Joanie was keeping herself busy in the kitchen, not wishing to interrupt this little confession session. 'Well, come on, then,' she invited. 'Tell me. It's your insecurity thing again, isn't it?'

'I guess it is,' sighed Gemma. 'They're not bad people, my friends, you know, only their parents seem to let them have their own way a lot more than Mum does me. I think we're old enough to make our own decisions.' She sounded a little defiant.

'Old enough to follow the crowd,' said Penny scornfully. 'If you were really mature, you'd make your own decisions, not let someone else make them for you. You've got to decide if you want to be a sheep or a shepherd.'

Gemma nodded, thinking hard. 'I wonder why Mum doesn't say it like that? She gets all emotional when she explains things.'

'She's nicer than me, that's why. She doesn't want to hurt your feelings.' Penny smiled as she bit into another sandwich. 'These are good, Gemma.'

Gemma sighed. 'Did you ever go into pubs? Things like that?'

'Certainly. But my dad told me to remember you're being watched. Suppose you go for a job, and someone has seen you behaving badly?' Penny paused. 'And suppose you went for a job, and that person had seen you walk away from doing something silly—how do you think you'd feel then?'

'Great.' Gemma edged nearer to Penny on the sofa and leaned her head on her shoulder. 'Penny, couldn't you stay on with Uncle Leo? I know our house isn't terribly posh, or anything, the stair carpet is fraying, and we need new curtains in the lounge—but——'

'If there's anyone I want to stay with it's you and Joanie, honestly,' Penny assured her. 'If I do go away to work, I'll come back and visit often. I want to see you become the *Herald*'s ace reporter!'

Joanie came in with a fresh pot of tea. She saw by their faces that the affair was closed. 'Thank you for putting Gemma in the picture.' She smiled at her daughter. 'Get clean cups, love.'

While Gemma obeyed, Joanie said, 'I heard her asking you to stay. Are you going to?'

'At Christmas I was sure I was going, everything was so unpleasant at the surgery. But now I really don't know.' Penny sipped her tea slowly. 'Anyway, Leo has probably put an advert in for someone else now.'

Joanie got up, and bustled about altering ornaments and plumping up cushions that didn't need it. 'In my opinion you'd both be making a mistake. It may be none of my business, but that man hasn't enjoyed life so much for a long time. He did miss you on Christmas Day —kept going all quiet and thoughtful. And you—you like being with him, I can tell. And you've got lots of real friends here. Do you really hate Liverpool so very much?'

'No, Joanie, I don't hate it at all.' Penny's voice was very quiet.

'Then I can't for the life of me see why you have to go.' Joanie picked up the tray and went off abruptly. Penny looked after her fondly.

Bathsheba came up, hoping for a walk. She rested her lovely head on Penny's knee, and looked at her with adoring eyes. Penny gazed back, her thoughts busy with what Joanie had implied. Leo missed her—maybe he did. But he still spent most of his time with Janet. Even to the point of taking a holiday together. That was something she could never live with. She stroked Bathsheba absently.

As she stroked, she reflected, 'I do love Leo. I'm wild with jealousy about Janet. It's love that's making life such a mixture of pleasure and pain. I'll never stop loving him. And she probably feels the same about him. I'm just a kid—why should I think I could get a man like Leo Zander? A mature man, a wise man—too good for a brat like me who can't even cook!' Putting it into words had been painful, but at least she understood herself now. She smiled sadly at the bitch. 'Bathsheba, it does hurt, you know.' And Bathsheba wagged her tail gently, as though she understood and sympathised.

The phone rang in the hall. Penny wasn't on duty, but she automatically sat up, pulled herself together mentally. 'Mrs Donaldson for you, Penny.'

'Thanks, Joanie.' She went through. 'Hello, Lil?'

'Oh, Penny, can you come, love? I've had a funny sort of haemorrhage.'

Penny had been afraid of this; the consultant had written to her. 'Are you still losing?' she asked.

'No. It was sort of sudden. I'm frightened, Penny!'

'Is Sam there?' Penny asked.

'Yes, but I didn't tell him. I mopped it up, then came to lie down—I told him I wanted a bit of a rest before getting the tea.'

'I'm on my way, dear. Don't worry.' And Penny hastily rinsed her face and brushed her teeth before making her way through the grey slush to the Donaldsons'.

She pretended it was a social call, to quieten any fears Sam might have. 'Sensible of you both, to take an afternoon nap. You stay there, Sam.' He was on the window seat. 'I'll just pop in and say hello to Lil.'

There was nothing abnormal to find when she examined Lil. 'I can't explain it, Lil. But you know I'll have to send you back to the gynae department? To Mr David?'

'I had a feeling you might.' Lil's round little face was resigned. 'He told me that the prolapse operation was a complete success, but somehow I could tell that he was keeping something back.'

Penny put her hand over Lil's, and nodded. 'Yes, he thought you might need more treatment later. I'll get you in quickly, and get it over, Lil.'

'It's all right, I've no qualms. He's such a kind man, Mr David. I know I'm in good hands.' As she drove to evening surgery, Penny couldn't help admiring the strong stoicism of the little lady, her calm acceptance of illness, once the initial fear had been overcome.

She turned the key in the surgery door, then she noticed there was a light in Leo's room, and called out to explain who she was. 'Only me, Leo. I have to admit Lil.'

He waited until she had made her call. As she looked up from her desk after putting the phone down, he was standing in the doorway, his tall figure shadowy in the half light of the dusk outside, and her little table lamp.

She said, 'You're early, Leo.'

'Janet chased me. She wants me back in good time, as she's invited some bridge cronies for drinks.' He came into the office and sat on the corner of her desk. 'Admit Lil, did you say? Lil Donaldson?'

'Yes. She's had a bleed PV and I wanted to catch Mr David before he went home.'

'I see. We knew there was likely to be further trouble?'

'Yes. He said in the letter that the prolapse operation should keep her happy from some months. This is a bit sudden for it to flare up again. It's a carcinoma—too far gone.'

Leo looked down, suddenly dejected. That wasn't like him; he usually kept his composure. But Lil and Sam

were very dear to him, she knew. She saw suddenly that
tears were glistening in his eyes, and she had an urge to
go to him, to comfort him. Yet who was she, to be so
bold? The little room was very quiet, just an occasional
car going past the window.

Leo took a deep breath, and turned to go away. Penny
watched his neat dark head, the set of his broad, elegant
shoulders. She remembered how she had felt a sort of
pity for his loneliness, even before she knew him as well
as she did now. That feeling returned. She yearned to
hold him in her arms, to be the one who could relieve his
awful loneliness and emptiness of life. But he had gone
now, and she heard him close his consulting room door
behind him.

Then Judy arrived, to unlock the waiting room for
evening surgery. Penny went back to her desk, her heart
raw with sympathy, with pity and with love. Judy tapped
on the door. 'I know it isn't time yet, but Mrs Watson
wants a word with you.'

'Okay, send her in, Judy.'

Mrs Watson not only came in, she cannoned in,
rushing up to Penny and throwing her arms round her
neck. 'Tim's all right, Doctor! He's out of intensive care.
They've just phoned me, and I'm going to see him!' Her
face was glowing with excitement. 'Oh, Doctor, I'm so
relieved! I never thought he'd be off those tubes and
things.'

'That's wonderful news,' smiled Penny. 'He's in an
ordinary ward?'

'Yes, C3. And he can come home when his weight is
normal.'

'What a wonderful new year gift for you!' said Penny
happily.

'Dr Harcourt, if you hadn't caught the disease when
you did, it might have been too late, mightn't it?'

'Yes, I think it would. But it was the Vicar who alerted
me. I take no credit.'

'But I thank you, Doctor, from the bottom of my heart.' Mrs Watson turned. 'I've got to run or I'll miss the bus. But I wanted to tell you—I never appreciated what a good man I had until I nearly lost him.'

Penny went through her quota of patients that evening with her usual efficiency, but all the time she was listening for Leo to leave the surgery early, to hurry back to Janet and their middle-class friends. She knew the sound of the Rover's engine as well as she knew her own. The thought of his dark head bent over his work haunted her as she worked. So this was what it was like, love . . . What a miserable state to be in!

He did go early. Penny stayed in her room, pretending to be busy. She heard Chris go out, and then Dai, who gave her a cheerful call. 'Okay, you little swot, you can go home now!'

''Night, Dai.' She stood up and took her sheepskin jacket from the hook. She walked slowly to the door, locked it after her, and went towards her lonely little Metro at the kerb. James Street tonight was peopled by ghosts—little Lil Donaldson and her bravery, Tim Watson and his fight for life. And that spectre of love that she would never forget—Leo turning towards her, holding out his arms, holding her to himself as though she were infinitely precious . . . People come, people go. Love comes, love goes. Penny felt that welcome cocoon of numbness, so familiar to those in her profession, who know that their natural human feelings are too sensitive to take it—and yet they go on taking it, year by year, day in day out . . . She was numb now, anaesthetised. She could go home and pretend that nothing was wrong.

The wind gusted suddenly. The sleet had stopped, and the night was fine. Penny drove slowly home the long way round. She drove along the Dock Road, past all the great historic names, now decaying and deserted—the Ellerman Line, the Huskisson Dock, Canada Lines. The Dublin night ferry was almost ready to sail, its great belly full of cars, the mouth still gaping, ready for more. It was a strange feeling. She felt part of this city now, fond of it, loyal to it. Yet fate had only set her here five months ago, and was planning to whisk her out again very shortly, with a broken heart and a good deal more common-sense.

The new Seaforth terminal was next, its tall modern lighting giving it a look of a stage set. But the only drama acted out that breezy night was a dance of the weeds, and the prowl of a dark secret cat. Penny drove past. She didn't want to go home yet; she knew where she was going, although she pretended she didn't until she was right down on the promenade car park, looking up at Leo Zander's house.

'Now this is crazy, spying on the man!' she told herself. She tried to pretend she had come down for the peace and quiet, and looked out to sea, where the tide was calm, the gusts occasionally whipping up the dark water into white horses. She got out of the car, leaned on the rail. The only other occupants of the car park were courting couples. She felt very alone.

And then she heard a door slam, and in spite of herself, she turned round and stared. Janet's house was lit up—every window. There was a string of big cars parked along the drive and out on the road. Penny got back in her car, rubbing her hands together to get some feeling back into them. She heard hearty voices greeting each other, as well-dressed couples made their way to Janet's front door.

She drove slowly past. Was Leo already inside, acting out the part of host with his usual debonair charm? She had passed the house now, but in her mirror she saw him; he had just walked from his own house. He walked slowly, with bent head. He was immaculate, in a dinner suit. He turned into Janet's drive, and she lost sight of him.

CHAPTER TWELVE

IT was Friday—Hogmanay, New Year's Eve. All four doctors would have liked to be off, but Penny had insisted on taking the calls. She had no engagements, and she wanted to keep busy, to keep her mind active, so that it had no time to pine. She spoke firmly to the others. 'There's no need to feel guilty, you know. I haven't any plans, and I'd like to be busy, okay?'

Chris said, with a look of gratitude, 'I know it should be my night. I'm really on call.'

She interrupted his excuses. 'And you have an invitation from some good friends in Preston. And why not? I'm here, and you can do my night when it comes. For goodness' sake, Chris—Lalla's been looking forward to this for months. You don't think I'm going to let you miss it, do you?'

Chris's black eyes were sincere. 'Thank you. Thank you very much.'

They had finished the morning surgery, and there was none in the evening. Chris left first. It was good that he wanted to get back to his family. He put his empty coffee cup on the tray, then he looked across the room at Penny. 'I have more than that to thank you for,' he said quietly.

She was embarrassed suddenly. She saw in his face a new and honest Chris. 'Don't be shy,' he told her. 'You had the guts to interfere, Penny. You saw that Lalla needed help, and you muscled in and gave it. I was too close to the picture to read it correctly.'

'Bull in a china shop,' admitted Penny.

'You did right.' Chris turned to the others. 'She saw it, I didn't—that I was trying to be British at work, Indian at home. It doesn't work. My wife has to live in this society, the same as me.'

'Forget it, Chris.' Penny didn't want any more confessions.

'I will. Except to say that I gave you more hassle than you deserve.' His face showed her that he was talking about the kisses that only she knew about. 'It would be nice if I started the new year on good terms with you.'

'Why not?' she smiled.

Leo said gently, 'You're embarrassing Penny.'

'Okay,' Chris smiled. 'So all the best to you all.'

Leo said, 'Wait a minute, Chris. Look, why don't you all come and have a drink with me tonight, before you go off and do your own thing? Chris?'

'Sure. We don't have to be in Preston all that early.'

'Dai?'

'Great, boss.'

'Penny?'

How could she refuse? 'Yes, naturally.' But her heart felt like lead. She couldn't stand more than ten minutes of Janet doing her perfect hostess act. She must pray that she had a call after that.

'Good. I'll get the receptionists too. We didn't have a party at Christmas, so a drink at New Year will be a fitting substitute.' Kay had just come in to get the cups, and she was enthusiastic about the invitation. 'Graham and I were only going to Judy and Bill's. It would be nice to come to you first, Doctor—specially because I was so grumpy over the party business. It was my bad temper——'

'No more guilty feelings, Kay. See you at about eight.'

'Okay, sir.'

Dai said after she'd gone, 'I'll be off too. But I've got something for you first, Leo,' and he took a folded piece of paper from his pocket. 'New year resolution number one—keep solvent!' It was a cheque for what he owed the surgery.

'I say—' Leo was beginning to thank him, but he interrupted, 'Now that's straightened out, come and see one of Nature's masterpieces. You too, Penny.' Chris had already gone.

Leo said, 'Don't tell me—you've bought another car!' But his tone was cheerful.

'Yes, Leo.'

'Then let's go and admire it, Penny.' Leo took his coat from the hook. 'Thanks for sorting things out, Dai.' The two men shook hands firmly, openly. Penny watched, feeling relieved that all the ill feeling, that had seemed so huge before Christmas, had sorted itself out so happily. Dai picked up his anorak and the three of them went to the front door together.

Dai opened it for the others. 'Penny, I hope you're not going to leave us, man. I don't feel like getting used to anyone else. I'm comfortable as we are, aren't you, Leo? We've grown accustomed to your face, *cariad*.'

'Oh, come on, Dai!' Penny had to joke, to stop herself showing her sudden emotion at his show of affection. 'I bet you say that to all the locums.'

'No—honest Welshman.'

They stopped in amazement at the kerb. Dai was standing with great pride beside a small ordinary-looking Mini. Leo demanded, 'What on earth is that?'

'A Mini, Leo. Never seen one before?'

'I can see that. But Dai, what about the image?'

'You mean you can't tell? Leo, this is *the* Mini—the souped-up engine, new racing tyres, customised exterior and super-plus luxurious interior with quadrophonic speakers. About the only thing this little beauty hasn't got is a machine gun!'

Leo turned to Penny, and they exchanged a smile. For a moment she had his full attention, and she gloried in it, before they turned their attention back to their colleague. 'What do you think?' asked Dai proudly.

Penny said cautiously, 'She's lovely, Dai. But can you sit upright?'

'Just watch me,' he grinned. His head cleared the roof by a full inch. 'See you guys tonight. All right to bring Andrea?'

'You know it's all right.'

Dai waved, and roared away from the kerb, waving a hand through the open sun roof. Penny and Leo watched as he disappeared down James Street.

They stood on the draughty pavement. Then Leo said, 'You're going to see Sam?'

'Yes. Mr David was operating this morning. I promised to let him know what they said.'

'The housekeeper—you'll have to tell——'

Penny said, 'I've already spoken to her. She's willing to come in full-time.'

'I seem to be always thanking you for what you do for the practice.'

'It's all right.'

'Thanks anyway.' He paused. 'You will come tonight?'

'I'll be there,' she promised.

'It was nice this morning, wasn't it? The four of us—do you know what I mean? And Kay and Judy?'

She understood. This practice, to her a passing job —to Leo it was his whole life, and to find the entire group of colleagues on friendly terms must have been heartwarming for him. She knew how he felt, as she stood next to him on that winter morning. So much in love . . . She took a step away from him. It was too easy to recall the night he had held her as though he would never let her go, but that was a lifetime away. 'Well, I'll see you later, then.' She wanted to say so much more, but there was no point. His bags were probably already packed for Paris.

She did the calls, pushing, as always, her personal thoughts far behind her. Joanie had a hot meal waiting when she got back for lunch. Patrick O'Hare was there too, an empty coffee mug before him. That was nice. She was glad that Patrick was being neighbourly; Joanie would need someone to chat to, when Penny had left.

'Where's Gemma?' she asked.

Patrick had gone back to work. Joanie said, 'She went out with Sharon and Carole. I let her go, Penny. But those girls aren't really the sort she ought to go around with.'

'Oh, Joanie, don't worry. As soon as school starts, she'll make a new set of friends. Meanwhile, trust to her conscience—she *has* got one! I'm sure she'll be all right.'

'But she hasn't been in for lunch, and it's after two,' worried Joanie.

'Did she say she'd be in for lunch?'

'No. But—oh, Penny, I thought things were getting easier, but they're not,' Joanie sighed.

They sat quietly in the kitchen. 'They won't get easier,' Penny told her. 'But you'll see—you'll be proud of that girl one of these days.'

'I like to think so.' Joanie smiled suddenly. 'Now, as you're daft enough to volunteer to be on call, you'd better put your feet up for an hour. You know we're due at Leo's tonight?'

'Yes. Do you want a lift?'

'No, thanks. You'll be on call, so Kay and Graham are picking us up.'

'I see.'

Penny went to lie down, but her thoughts were jumbled and active. She kept thinking of Lil, probably just off the operating table. Leo was going to take Sam later on, when she had come round. Poor souls! Yet it happened—to so many people. Everyone had done their best. She recalled Leo's tears, and felt her own eyes wet at the sadness and inevitability of misfortune, and of love . . . .

Gemma returned home at four. Penny was just getting up, after deciding that she couldn't sleep. She heard Joanie's shrill, 'Gemma, where have you been until this hour?'

'Out.'

There was a silence, then Joanie said, her tone now calm, and an octave lower, 'I'm sorry—I should have asked you if you'd be back for lunch. Try to call me next time, love.'

Gemma said, 'Actually, I did try to ring you, but the boxes in town were all out of order. All the ones along the Kings Road are vandalised.'

'It's all right.' Penny was proud of Joanie's self-restraint then. 'Come and have a bite to eat. We're invited to Uncle Leo's tonight, so you don't want to spoil your appetite.'

'Oh, great news, Mum! Is Penny coming? Can I wear that new blouse, do you think, or is it too summery?'

'You can wear it with a jacket over the top.'

'And will you lend me your pink earrings?' asked Gemma.

'Yes, all right, if you lend me your gold link bracelet.'

'Oh, sure. I'll be wearing something much more modern. Can I see what Penny's wearing?'

'She's asleep,' her mother told her.

'I'm awake now,' called Penny. 'But I've got a couple of calls to do.'

Gemma burst in, her face flushed, looking happy and pretty. 'You're coming to Uncle Leo's with us? What time will you be back?'

'Before seven. That gives you three hours to bathe and get ready. Is it long enough?'

She giggled. 'Has Uncle Leo got any more videos for me?'

'I have no idea.'

'I bet he has!'

Penny drove to Winslow Court in the swirling wind.

The first floor flats were boarded up because of vandalism, making the place look derelict. The hoardings were plastered with posters for pop groups, for protest political meetings, for permanent strike calls and marches. Bits of torn posters fluttered around her ankles, as she parked as close to the entrance as she could, to avoid the stinging wind.

She ran up the stairs to Debbie's flat. She was used to the smell now, to the crude graffiti scrawled on the walls. She stopped at the door, still badly in need of a decent coat of paint, and found herself suddenly surprised and delighted by the small circlet of silver leaves and plastic holly hanging from the knocker. It lit up the dank landing, a small beacon of hope and optimism in a waste land.

She rang the bell. At first there was no answer, so she rang again, and tapped on the door with her knuckles. This time the door was wrenched open, and she heard an oath as it snagged against a fold in the carpet. Penny braced herself for a family quarrel.

But it was just the opposite. 'Come along in, Dr Harcourt. It's real nice of you to come out on a day like this.' Mr Grant straightened the carpet. His oath had been against the carpet, not against Penny.

'I just thought I'd pop in. I've brought a little something for Jamie.'

Debbie came into the tiny hall, young Jamie in her arms, looking plump and flushed, his hair tousled. 'I'm sorry we didn't realise it were the bell, Doctor. We was having a game with the baby—we were laughin' that much we didn't 'ear. It's his playtime, y'see.' Then she said, as Penny touched Jamie's little cheeks, and won a smile from him, 'There isn't anything wrong, is there?' Her face changed. 'The hospital haven't written?'

'No, nothing like that. But your mother has written to change doctors, and I thought I'd make sure everything was all right.'

Mr Grant gave a gruff shout of laughter. 'That's nowt, Doctor. She's shoved off with another bloke—her boss from the Bingo. Moved in with him over Toxteth way—that's why she's changing. Much good it'll do her!'

Debbie showed Penny into the living room. 'We don't really notice much difference, to be honest, Doctor. She wasn't here much.' She set Jamie down to play with toys littered over the floor. 'But I got a book about cooking for health—look.' She handed Penny a well thumbed cookery book. 'I've done all them what I've marked.'

Her father came and sat down. 'She's good, y'know. Those frozen things—they're full of artificial stuff, y'know. You never know what they're trying to stuff down your throat. Our Deb uses all proper indigents, like it says.' They were both enthusiastic about their new life. And Jamie looked very contented; Penny lifted him up, and listened to his chest with her stethoscope. Then she pulled down his little vest and jumper—both comparatively clean and fresh.

'Deb, you're working miracles!' she smiled. 'Jamie is one of our star babies, you know. We're all terribly impressed by the way you've seen him over his troubles. He's doing very well indeed.'

'Well, I watch his vitamins. And me dad bought one of them blender things with his last Giro cheque, so I can make proper fruit juice. It's great.' Debbie beamed at Penny's praise. 'Doctor, d'you think when he's a bit older, I could train to look after children? Other children?'

'Why not? Go and get some brochures from the careers office at Bootle Tech.' Debbie was a caring girl, and her love for her baby had helped her to grow up and trust to her own maternal instincts. Penny felt a warmth of pleasure at the success story before her. And she recalled the despair and the anger she had felt when she first met this family.

'Well, Jamie, here's another toy to throw around the floor.' She took out the fluffy teddy bear dressed in Liverpool football gear. 'I hope it's the right team!' and the baby picked it up, and cuddled his nose into the soft fur.

Penny ran downstairs, her feet light after the sight she had left. She had learned not to react to the externals. This might be a poor area, but the richness of love had not passed all of it by.

But her philosophical thoughts took a nasty jolt when she came out of the flats. Two black youths were standing by her car. Last time the radio had been taken. Her heart quivered slightly. Did she stay hidden, or face them boldly? She had no money with her. She stood for a second, but it was far too cold for standing, and she raised her chin boldly and walked firmly towards the car.

One of the lads turned, and under the yellow street lamp, she recognised him. 'Billy Mackie—How are you, Billy?'

The other boy turned too. Penny didn't know him, but if he was with Billy, it was all right. Billy was a patient, just out of hospital after a repair of a torn ligament.

Billy smiled a big white smile. 'I knew it were your car, Doctor—I recognised the number.' He spoke with a broad nasal Liverpool accent. 'I thought me an' Zeke 'd hang about, keep an eye on it, like. You can't be too careful round 'ere. Some of these lads 'd 'ave yer knicker elastic soon as look at yer!'

'I'm very grateful,' Penny smiled at them. 'Happy New Year.'

'Happy New Year to you. It'll be happier when I'm allowed to play footie again,' Billy added.

'Ah, that won't be this season, I'm afraid. But they'll tell you when you go back to the clinic.'

'I know. I'm not bothered, so long as it's getting better.'

Penny got into the car. 'Thanks very much for keeping an eye. Take up darts, Billy,' she advised.

'I might. But with my luck I'd get tennis elbow!'

She drove away, again remembering how bitter and upset she had felt the first time she had called at Winslow Court. The wind buffeted the car, but she hardly noticed it, as she reflected how proud she was of Debbie, how lucky she was to have patients like Billy. The meanness of the streets, the poverty of the people, never entered her mind. Inside their homes, inside their hearts, was neither meanness nor poverty, but great riches.

It was when she was dressing to go to Leo's New Year drinks party that the real discomfort started. She hated the idea of Janet Rhys-Evans being there, queening it over Leo, doing her Lady Bountiful bit.

Yet Gemma was so excited, and Joanie's eyes were sparkling as she prinked in front of the mirror at her new short hairstyle. Penny could never spoil their fun. So she obediently put on her best cream wool dress, and added a scarlet scarf, shoes and earrings. 'Will that do, Gemma?' she asked.

Gemma jumped up importantly. 'Mmm, very nice, Penny. You see, you can look gorgeous when you want. Your hair needs fluffing up a bit. Sit still.' And she duly fluffed up Penny's short style into a fashionable shape. 'It's a really pretty colour, you know. Now, these loose necklines are supposed to be pulled down revealing one bare shoulder . . .'

'Don't you dare! Nothing of mine is being revealed, thank you very much.' Penny pulled up the neckline, rearranged the scarf—and threw a cushion at Gemma. 'Come on, I'll give you a lift. Kay will take you home if I have a call.' As she very much hoped she would. She was dreading the evening.

The wall lights were on, she could tell from the front drive. Subdued lighting, gentle background music—oh yes, Janet was very good at that. So discreet, so very tasteful . . . Penny was so very jealous. Gemma ran up the steps and rang the bell enthusiastically.

But it was Leo who answered—Leo alone, in a perfectly fitting grey lounge suit over a tailored grey silk shirt. He looked so dashing, so terribly handsome and desirable. 'Hey, Uncle Leo, that's real cool!' Gemma reached up and kissed him. 'Thanks ever so much for inviting us.'

'It's my pleasure. And yes, I did get the videos you asked for.'

Joanie went in before Penny, who pretended she hadn't locked the car door, as an excuse for not seeing Janet quite so quickly. But she couldn't put off the moment, so she went up the step, took Leo's outstretched hand, and felt his warm breath on her cheek as he gave her the tiniest of kisses. 'You're looking very lovely. Any calls this afternoon?'

'One. It's been very quiet.'

'It always is, thank goodness.'

Penny went into the long lounge. Yes, the lights were as she expected, the music was Mozart . . . but there was no Janet. She must be putting on the warpaint, thought Penny grimly.

'May I go through to the study, Uncle Leo?' asked Gemma.

'Don't you want a glass of champagne first?'

'No, thanks.'

'I'd better go with her—make sure she knows how to work that thing.' But Joanie accepted a glass of wine to take with her.

Leo looked across at Penny, as she sat uncomfortably on the edge of her chair. 'Do you want to watch videos too?' he asked.

She smiled and shook her head.

'Do you think we've been left alone on purpose?'

Penny looked scared. 'What on earth for?'

'I think they want me to ask you to stay on at the surgery.'

'Oh.' She had been clutching the cold glass as though it were a weapon. If they were going to talk about her future, then perhaps she could talk naturally—tell him about her growing attachment to the patients, ask for a little more time to make up her mind. She took a sip of champagne, and relaxed a little. 'Leo—I was hoping——'

At that moment the bell pealed. 'Damn,' muttered Leo. 'Why do they have to come so early?'

'It'll be Janet. You'd better hurry.'

He stood up. 'Janet isn't coming. She's doing some last-minute packing, and then she wants an early night.' He went to the door, leaving his junior partner feeling distinctly happier about the whole evening. Yet—packing? Was the Paris trip so very close, then? Why wasn't Leo packing? He came back with Dai and Andrea. 'And anyway, Penny, I didn't invite her,' he added firmly.

There was no time for more, as Dai swept in and took the floor. 'She likes the car,' he told them happily. 'I always say any woman can be bowled over by a ride in a Porsche. It takes a real connoisseur to appreciate a little gem like mine.'

Andrea giggled. 'Well, I'm small myself. This cuts down the competition, because he can't invite anyone over five foot ten!'

Chris and Lalla had the children with them. The little girl was delighted to run off and watch the pop videos with Gemma, while the baby slept in Lalla's arms. 'It would be nice to see the new year in with you all,' said Lalla, smiling charmingly, 'but these friends are very close, and we do not see them very often.'

'I understand.' Leo was standing in the middle of the room, welcoming guests as they arrived, looking very much in charge. 'As the party was only arranged this afternoon, I'm flattered that you all took the trouble to accept.'

Dai called from the drinks table, 'Well, we have to keep well in with the boss, man!'

There was general laughter. Chris said, 'Yes, Dai, I can see you aren't enjoying yourself at all!'

Penny found herself chatting to Graham, Kay's quiet husband. They looked around to see everyone relaxed and in a good mood. Graham confided, 'Kay's been through a bad patch this year. She reckons it was you that helped her over it.'

'Friends,' Leo was looking around, and the room fell quiet, 'I know you all have other engagements. I know what I'm saying doesn't really need saying, because you all know it. But it's been a funny sort of year. A lot of things went wrong, at one time or another—and some things went right.' He looked across at Penny, and smiled slightly. She hoped he would not embarrass her by mentioning her in front of everyone. 'Now Chris and Lalla have to get off to Preston, so here's the toast now, and it comes with all the sincerity I have. Whatever has happened in the year—it was good to live through it with you. We've made it—and made it smiling. Here's to the next—I look forward to it. Happy New Year, everybody.'

And suddenly they all stood, repeated his words, and clinked glasses with everyone within reach. Penny found herself suddenly choked, unable to say the words as they were said to her. Was she part of this or not? Because she knew she wanted to be, very much. Could she really walk away at the end of February, as she had planned —leave this family of assorted characters with whom she had shared so much, received so much?

Lalla was at her side. 'Penny, I have to thank you. I know I've done it before, but life has really turned the corner for us. We are like newlyweds!' She put a hand on Penny's arm. 'We must go now. But Penny, please think again about leaving the practice. Chris says they couldn't have a nicer partner.'

The phone rang, and Penny put up a hand. 'It's all right—probably for me.' And she was suddenly annoyed. She was enjoying Leo's party and she didn't want to leave it just at this stage. 'Dr Harcourt?'

'The name's O'Leary, Doctor. You saw me mam last week.'

'Yes. She's going for investigations for a possible duodenal ulcer.'

'S'right. Well, she's in a lot of pain, and the pills you gave her aren't doing any good.'

'How much is a lot?' It was so easy to get stomach-ache during a season of over-eating and over-drinking.

'Terrible bad. Stomach and chest, and her neck's hurting too.'

'I'll come along. What's the address again?' asked Penny.

Leo was standing behind her in the hall, where Lalla and Chris were collecting the children. 'You have to go?' he asked.

'Yes. Sounds like an infarct—she's had the pain for two hours.'

He opened the door for her. 'Shall I go?'

'Of course not.'

'Penny—you will come back?' he asked urgently.

'Yes, all right.' He stood and watched her as she got in the car, checked that she had all her instruments, drug bag and prescription pad. She saw him outlined in the door, as she drove away, and she looked into the mirror, to get one last glimpse of him. How dear he was! And how close to going away with his glamorous neighbour . . .

It wasn't a heart attack, but Mrs O'Leary had a bad attack of angina. Penny stayed with her until she was completely satisfied that the pain had gone. 'Stay where you are for two days,' she directed. 'I'll make an urgent medical appointment as soon as hospital out-patients opens again on the second. But phone me at once if there's any more pain.'

She drove back along the dock road. The pubs were all lit up tonight, the people showing no signs of depression, of deprivation. Tonight Liverpool was showing how gutsy it was, how optimistic—maybe next year would bring a job, a house, some hope . . .

She had parked in Leo's drive before she realised that the house was very quiet. Had everyone gone? She hesitated before ringing the bell, but Leo had seen her, and had opened the door. 'Come in, Penny. You didn't finish your champagne.'

'It wasn't an infarct, but she does have heart trouble. I must remember to make an appointment for her . . .' her voice tailed off, as they went into the lounge. She felt suddenly afraid. There was no reason for her to be here; she didn't want to be here alone with him.

'There was a call from Sam. He's spending the night at the hospital.' Leo's voice was grave. 'I don't think it will be long. And without Lil, Sam won't last.'

They were both silent. There was no need for words. Sam and Lil—together all their lives. There would only be a short separation, and then they would be together again.

'What are you thinking?' He handed her a glass of champagne.

'I thought Janet might have popped in to wish you the compliments of the season.'

'Not her. Would you if you were flying to Agadir tomorrow morning?'

Penny swallowed her champagne quickly, before she chocked. 'Agadir? *The* Agadir? In the North Africa?'

'That's the one. She goes every January for three months. We suspect she has a thing going with the manager of the hotel.'

'Agadir——' Penny repeated.

'Don't go on saying that. We have a problem to solve.'

'Leo, why are you so good to Joanie?' she asked suddenly.

'Because Gemma was born in this house—when Joanie was looking after Mother. I honestly believe that the father went away because Joanie wouldn't leave Mother.'

It all seemed so ridiculously simple. 'You knew the father?' she asked.

'Yes. He was terribly fond of Joanie. Nice chap—bit immature. He went to Canada, and Joanie wouldn't go. Gemma was born—and we all loved her like one of the family.' Leo smiled suddenly. 'She's not a bad kid even now, but she was a darling baby. I'm fond of babies.'

Penny put down her glass, and Leo refilled it. 'Leo, I'm still on call!' she protested.

'No, you aren't. I phoned the Liverpool locums. We're employing them for the next twenty-four hours.' He sat opposite to her, on the edge of the chair, not totally at ease. 'Any more questions, Penny?'

She took another sip. It made her head feel delightfully unreal. In a few short minutes Leo had shattered all her doubts, all the reasons she had for not staying on. 'Just one.' She was suddenly frightened to mention it. 'Would you—will you—let me—stay on with the practice?'

Leo didn't reply. Penny's head was down, so she didn't see his face, but she heard him put his glass down carefully on the side table. Then he stood up and went to the window, his back towards her. 'I dare say that can be arranged.' Something had happened to his voice.

She raised her head. She looked at him as he stood, one arm up against the window frame, looking out. 'Leo?' She put her glass beside his and followed him to the window. 'Leo?' she asked very softly.

He turned towards her. There were tears in his eyes. And this time she didn't hesitate at all, but threw her arms around his neck. 'Darling Leo, don't cry!' He caught her with a violence that almost winded her, but exhilarated her at the same time. They clung together as though their very lives depended on not letting go. It was so wonderful and magical, that he did need her, that he did want her, that she was the one who could take away his loneliness.

After a long time, he let her move fractionally away from him. His hair was dishevelled, and he loosened his tie and threw it on the window seat. 'I'd better draw the curtains,' he whispered, his voice boyish and vulnerable. He pulled the cord, and the curtains swished together. Penny sat beside him on the window seat, and he took both her hands, looking into her face with brown eyes that had adoration in them, and no secrets at all. She looked back, hardly daring to believe what she read in his face.

'I can't really believe this is me,' she whispered, with a little grin. 'But if it's a dream, I hope I don't wake up!'

'Look—we'd better get this straightened out.' Leo was smiling and embarrassed and flushed all at the same time. 'You—well, you seem to quite like me?'

'I love you with so much of myself that there's nothing left!'

'Darling!' he lifted her hands to his lips, and she wiped away the traces of tears on his eyelashes. 'No, I'm not going to kiss you again until it's all clear and spelt out in words of one syllable—my head's swimming too much to understand any more. You'll stay with the practice?'

'I will.'

'And you'll come to Paris with me?'

'I will.'

'Just like that?' he quirked an eyebrow at her.

'One week with you is worth more than a lifetime with anyone else,' Penny assured him. 'When?'

He laughed, as though he could scarcely believe what she was saying. 'My love, on our wedding day, of course.

You don't think we could face the patients with no marriage lines?'

She looked down. 'Weddings take some organisation. And Leo—I don't know how to cook.'

'That's terribly serious!' he agreed gravely.

'Are you laughing at me?'

'A bit.' He stood up, and pulled one curtain back. 'Look, Penny, it's next year out there.' He drew her into his arms, laughing a little as he pulled her close. 'And I don't think my feet will come down to earth for most of it!' She slipped suddenly from his arms. 'Hey, come back! Where are you going, darling?'

'I just want to phone Mum. Can I?'

'Of course.'

'I have to tell her she can go and buy that suit,' Penny explained.

'Tell her what you like. And give her my love. And then come back to me very quickly, because I love you too much to be able to spare you for any longer.'

Penny did as he asked.